Argentine Mist

A Nicholas Chambers Mystery

By Christopher J. Dacey

Dedicated to

Suzanne, Connor, Madison, & Aidan

2nd Edition

Table of Contents

The rain tapped steadily on the window of my fifth floor corner office. October 16, 1941 had started off routine enough. The radio had predicted rain all day, all night, and maybe all weekend. There was a Nor'easter headed up the coast from the Carolina's, which had made its way to New England. The surf down by the beaches was already kicking up, and since it was Friday most businesses were letting their people out early. I lit my last cigarette, glanced out the window at the steady downpour, and quickly dismissed the thought of walking over to the five and dime for a new pack of Lucky's. It had been one of those unusually wet weeks, and I was beginning to forget what the sun looked like.

I walked over to the window facing Weybossett Street and looked down at the umbrellas dotting the sidewalk below me. Crowds of people beneath them were rushing on their way home from work. They looked like black whirlwinds moving to and for protecting the earthly creatures below them. The rain was falling hard and steady and the street had transformed itself into a small river now. The river was running down the sidewalks and into the gutters at a good clip in the direction of Narragansett Bay. I cracked the window a couple of inches. A wet salty breeze shoved its way into my office.   It was one of those storms where you could smell the salt air blowing off the Bay. My office was about a half a mile or so from the ocean, but the rain always seemed to carry the sea air into the city.

Across the street, a red figure appeared with no whirlwind protecting it, and began making its way through the crowd. She crossed the street and stepped onto the sidewalk below. Just then a large truck barreled by, dousing her with muddied gutter water. She shook off like a wet dog and turned to note the address on my building. I noticed she glanced over her shoulder for a moment, looking back across the street and then quickly disappeared through the main lobby door below.

The day so far had been uneventful. I woke up late and had breakfast at the Broad Street Diner around 10:00am. I had a meeting at 11:00am with an old client who called yesterday to say he was in desperate need of my services again. He never showed. At lunchtime I grabbed a quick sandwich at the pharmacy across the street and bumped into my second grade teacher, Sister Barbara. She seemed to have kept tabs on most of my former classmates, and talked my ear off for almost an hour.   The highlight of my day was a call I received after lunch from the local church asking for a donation to help build a garage for the new school bus. I was feeling charitable so I pledged a dollar. Since then I had been rationing my cigarettes and watching the rain pound the street below. I would have closed up shop after lunch if I hadn't received that call at 2:00pm. She sounded desperate and wanted to see me right away. I suggested she come by on Monday, but she insisted that it would be too late. I finally gave in and told her to come right down, but that was over three hours ago.

I heard the elevator open at the end of the hallway, followed by the echo of clicking footsteps on the tarnished marble hallway outside my office. Shortly after, I heard three light knocks on my office door. I strolled out into my reception area and walked past the empty receptionist desk. It had been empty for several months now, ever since my last girl Pauline had eloped with the building superintendent. Since business was slow, I decided to do my own reception. I could see a silhouette of a woman now through the frosted plate glass of my outer office door, which read *Nicholas Chambers, Private Investigation*. I walked to the door and opened it. She looked to be around twenty-five, five feet eight inches in height, a brunette with a figure that probably got a lot of looks. She gave me a faint smile. The muddied overcoat was folded over her arms now. She wore a red blouse with a black skirt that rose more than a few inches above her knee. The only thing covering her legs was a layer of grimy gutter water. She wore a jet black felt hat with yellow trim on the side. "Mr. Chambers?" she asked in exasperated tone. "Yes" I replied. Won't you come in Miss Baxter?" She dripped into my reception area and followed me on into the office.

I asked her to have a seat in the easy chair across from my desk, and I pulled up a small chair and sat beside her. Her face was flushed and she was drenched from head to toe. "I don't want to give you the wrong impression, but could I offer you a drink to warm you up? I have some scotch in the desk?" I don't usually offer clients a drink the first time I meet them, but she just looked like she needed one. "Why thanks, if it's not too much trouble Mr. Chambers. I got a little lost and had to walk a few blocks in this rain …and thanks again for seeing me on such short notice". I walked over to the sideboard and poured her a shot of scotch, then handed the glass over to her. She downed the shot, I did a second take, and we got down to business.

"So what brings you here?" I asked. She opened her purse and gingerly pulled out an old tattered photograph. She glanced at me for a moment without saying anything and then spoke up, "Before I get into any details with you Mr. Chambers, I need to know if things will be kept in strict confidence, … I mean, … will what I tell you be protected like with attorneys and their clients?" She looked up at me with look that seemed a little too helpless for the outfit she was wearing. I thought it over for a moment, rubbed my chin a little and then replied

"I'll always do my best Miss Baxter, but if what you tell me involves me in some crime or conspiracy, I can't make any promises. With that said if you're asking whether I take some heat for a while, well… I usually can if the client has been honest with me." Her eyebrow rose somewhat and she shot me a doubtful glare. "I guess that will have to do since I can't wait any longer" she replied. She pulled a small photo from her purse and gazed down at it for a moment. Just then I noticed a single tear begin to roll its way down the curve of her face. She didn't bother to wipe it away as she dropped her head down.

After a few seconds she spoke up "This is a picture of my sister Allison" she said as she handed the photo over to me. "I haven't seen her in three weeks, and I want you to find her." The photo was of a young woman with long brown hair and a dark complexion. Her hair was pulled back into a pony tail, and tied with a white ribbon in back. She wore a plaid skirt and a plain power blue shirt. She had a scarf wrapped around her narrow neck. The picture was taken on the front steps of a small cape, and the girl was seated with a small shabby looking chocolate dachshund by her side. The dog had sympathetic eyes, and a light brown beard around his mouth. The house was modest in appearance with overgrown shrubs and a small statue of the Virgin Mary on the front lawn. The lawn was neglected, and the gray paint on the house and front stairway was peeling badly.

I looked back at her and asked the two questions I always ask in missing persons cases, "How old is your sister, and when did you last see her?" She lifted her head, and I could see the tracks of several tears that had cut through her mascara and made their way down her face. "She is twenty-one... We met downtown for coffee about three weeks ago." She replied. "Allison works at the Journal as a research assistant for a Mr. Thompson, and I work in the Industrial Bank building. We always meet for coffee every Tuesday on our lunch breaks down at the Beacon Diner on Allen's Ave. Two weeks ago she didn't show up so I called her apartment that night, but no one answered. "You said no one? Is she married or does she have a roommate?" I piped in. "No, she's single... lives alone in a small second floor apartment on the East Side" she replied with a look of annoyance. She went on "The next day I called her employer and was told she hadn't been at work at all that week. She hasn't shown up for work since that time, and I am really getting worried at this point. I think something might have happened to her." She looked up at me with an apprehensive glance. I stood up, paced the room a little, and questioned her "Miss Baxter, have you tried to contact any other family members who may have seen or spoken with her?" "Please call me Jill, Mr. Chambers" she replied. "Actually, Allison and I are the only family living in Rhode Island. Most of our family leaves in New York. I contacted our parents in Brooklyn and they haven't seen her since she visited them in May. I'm afraid I may have worried them with my call." She started to cry more openly now.

The rain had picked up and was really drumming a beat against the window now. Darkness had begun to envelop the City, and the knocking of streetcars below had begun to subside. I grabbed at the empty cigarette case on my desk, and tossed it back down in frustration. I stood up and walked back to the oak sideboard and poured her another drink. I turned towards her and questioned "How about the police?" Why I asked, I don't know since that remark was generally not good for business. She looked up and straightened her face suddenly, wiping a few tears from her eyes "I would rather not involve the police for personal reasons Mr. Chambers, and I can't elaborate on those reasons right now" she replied as she reached down to open her purse. I could see her face change. The sympathetic distraught face disappeared almost instantly, while her demeanor took on a more businesslike approach. She pulled a c-note out of her purse and held it tightly in her hand. I shook my head and thought it over. Something about her didn't sit right with me, but the hundred dollar bill in her hand did. Her voice began to crack a little "If

I could go to the police, I wouldn't be here... but I am here so that should tell you something. If you don't want to help me, then ok. I'll find someone who will" She said as she began to rise out of her chair. I stood up "Look here Miss Baxter, nobody said anything about not wanting to help, but I need to know my clients are playing straight with me. You'll need to give me a little more than that to go on." What type of trouble was your sister in?" I probed.

She sat back down in silence. I saw her glance around the room, surveying the old furniture, dusty drapes, and empty sidebar. Perhaps she was deciding whether I was disreputable and hungry enough to tell her story to. After a few moments she began "My sister started dating a man about six months ago named Johnny... Johnny Corrao. I only met him once, but she talked like it was getting pretty serious. I can't say for sure, but I think he may have been connected or something, well you know what I mean. Anyway, she would never directly involve herself in any kind of trouble, but I guess I'm worried she may have gotten in with the wrong crowd."

I knew who Johnny Corrao was, and so did most people who read the papers. I walked over to side bar, and poured myself a scotch. "Is that it?" "Yes Mr. Chambers, that's all I know. She really didn't talk much about him" she replied. I looked back at her "My fee is $20 a day, plus expenses". She handed me the c-note and told me to hold it as a deposit. I turned around and stashed the bill in an old cigar box that I kept in my top desk drawer. "Well, I'll see what I can do, leave me your telephone number". She smiled and replied "Williams-7186 I appreciate all your help Mr. Chambers, and please contact me directly as soon as you hear anything". I jotted her number down on a pad, and we both stood up from our seats. I walked over and opened the office door for her "Well, you'll hear from me... If you don't mind I'll hold onto the picture for a while, and please call me if you hear from your sister in the meantime". "Thank you again Mr. Chambers" she said as she walked out the front office door. I watched her as she strolled slowly away from me down the empty corridor. Somehow, I felt she knew I was watching.

2: Drive by Night.

I left my office at half past six. It was dark now.
The rain was really pouring down and the wind had
picked up. They were getting ready to close over at
the five and dime, but I needed a couple of packs for
the weekend. As I approached the door, the clerk
inside was just about to flip the "closed" sign over.
I slipped through the door and he flipped the sign
over just the same, locking it behind me. "You just
made it bud, what'll it be?" I shook off like a damp
cat and walked up to the counter, he followed
closely behind. "I'll take a pack of Lucky's, and
what are they saying about the weather?" He
fumbled behind the counter for a minute and then
emerged with a pack of Chesterfield. "All out of
Lucky Strike, but I have Chesterfield. If you want
them that will be ten cents Jack, and you can listen
for yourself" he replied as he turned up the volume
up on the radio. I heard the static voice reporting
*"….Most downtown business have closed early for the
evening to allow workers to get home before the storm
arrives in force. The national weather bureau in Boston
is predicting 50 mile an hour winds with heavy rains and
street flooding…"* "Sounds like a real blow. Could
you give me a paper with that?" He laughed "All
sold out at noon today, must be cause of the storm."
I gave him the dime and he let me go without much
conversation.

I could see the lights of the store turning off behind

me as I crossed to the other side of the street. It was just then that I noticed the entire city street was darkened and I seemed to be its only inhabitant. The city looks so different at night, and right now it was looking pretty dark and ominous. A few dimly lit street lights dotted along the street. My car was parked a few blocks from the office. I had a deal with Miller's Grocery to park behind his store. A year ago, he needed some business taken care of and I took care of it for him. Since then I had a permanent parking space and all the free milk I could drink.

I ran for cover making my way from one doorway to the next as the rain seemed to be getting even heavier and the winds much stronger. I wondered how she had made out traveling back several blocks in this downpour. After a couple of blocks I was totally drenched and gave up on the doorways. I strolled to the corner where the grocery store was and took a right turn down the alley into the back lot. I spotted my 1938 Oldsmobile coupe through the downpour. It was parked just where I had left it that morning. I stopped short suddenly when I noticed a dim light flicker inside. I ducked quickly into a doorway overhang and hugged the side of the building, standing completely still. The rain seemed very loud to me now, and was the only sound I could hear. The alley was dark and deserted. I stood still and kept my eye on the car in the back of the lot. There it was again, a small light inside the car that now appeared to be the burn of a cigarette. Someone was waiting for me.

I instinctively reached under my lapel for my gun, even though I knew I hadn't brought it that day. I glanced over to the loading dock and spotted an axe handle leaning against a stool. I crouched down and crawled slowly to the shipping platform and picked it up. I decided to make my way along the rear of the building and approached the car from the opposite direction. If someone was waiting for me, they would be expecting me to stroll down the side street directly towards my car. Maybe he hadn't seen me in this rain, and I might still have a chance to get the jump on him. I stayed low to the ground, feeling more and more like a wet cat as I made my way along the back fence towards my car. I stopped about four feet from the car to see if I could make anyone out. The rain was so strong and loud, I could barely see the silhouette of a man in the front passenger seat, and the slow burn of the cigarette in his mouth. The same thought kept running threw my head as I watched the rain hammer the roof of my car. Did he have a gun? Just then an idea suddenly flashed through my head and I sprang towards the car without thinking if it was a smart idea. I swung the axe handle clear threw the passenger window, shattering the glass into fragments. The occupant in the front seat fell back on his right side as I jerked the car door open and dragged him out by his collar. He was either shocked or dazed because he didn't put up much of a struggle. Soon, he was face down in a puddle of muddy rain water, as I pressed the axe handle into his spine and pulled his head back by his hair.

"What gives pal?" He didn't respond, aside from a low groan. I must have made contact with his head judging by the blood dripping down from his left temple. I reached into his jacket pocket and pulled his wallet out. He had three dollars and twenty cents, but no identification. A snub nosed revolver was tucked inside his pants belt, which I helped myself to. I pulled a small piece of folded paper out from inside of his wallet. I looked down at the semi-conscious figure. He looked to be in his early thirties, large build, over six feet and maybe two hundred and forty pounds. His hair was dark and his clothing showed some wear. His face had disappeared into the puddle and he began to choke on rain water. I did my best to drag him by his arms towards the rear of the store, then made my way to the loading dock and dropped him down like a sack of potatoes. He let out another low groan as his head slammed against the concrete. Under the dim light of the loading dock I got a better look at his face. I recognized him instantly, It was Vincent "the hammer" Palaeno. He was a minor player in the Providence underworld, and had a reputation as a hard-nosed collector. Rumor had it he got his nickname when he took a sledge hammer to some poor sap's car who had parked in his usual spot. I opened the folded paper which read *1030 Warwick Neck Drive*. I knew the area. It was about fifteen miles south of the city along the coast. "Get up" I shouted as my foot made contact with his ribs. He just groaned and rolled over. I must have hit him a litter harder than I thought.

I walked back to my car and opened the trunk, and pulled out some rope and a pair of handcuffs that I always kept around for special occasions like this. I closed the trunk and started back towards the loading dark. It took me a few minutes to tie his feet together. I cuffed one of his hands to the iron rail on the loading dock, and gave him a more thorough search now, but still came up empty. I'd place an anonymous call to the police in the morning to come and pick him up. There was bound to be some outstanding warrant for him, his type always did.

I hurried back to my car and opened the trunk. I had an old blanket in there that I used to jerry rig around the door frame to slow the rain gusts from soaking the inside of my car. I jumped into a very wet front seat, started the engine and drove off. It took me about fifteen minutes to get on Post Road, and I headed south for Warwick. The rain was really pouring down now, and it was difficult to see the road in front of me. The blanket covering my broken window was rapidly loosing its battle with nature. I drove for nearly twenty-five minutes and only saw one other truck, which passed me going northbound. No one was out in this blow, no one with any sense at least.

I pulled a smoke from my jacket and thought about the thug I had left tied up, and tried to connect him to an old case. Why was he waiting for me? He was clearly hired muscle sent to deliver a message, deliver me somewhere, or maybe just to deliver a bullet. Could be anybody really, but I didn't like the idea of someone trying to get the jump on me. I was able to surprise him, and needed to find out as much as I could before the person or persons who hired him realized their boy hadn't come through for them. The thought of his needing medical attention entered my mind for a moment, and then quickly departed. My thoughts began to drift to the girl, her concern for her sister, and her boyfriend Johnny Corrao. I had dealt with these type of cases in the past, and most of the time it turned out the missing person was drowning their sorrows in a bar somewhere, or having a fling with someone the family disapproved of. Generally, I didn't work missing person's cases, but business had been slow and her legs had persuaded me to help out.

I took a left onto Occupatuxet Rd, drove by the airport and headed into the village of Connimicut, which was clearly deserted. I saw a barber shop and a small diner, both of which had closed signs in their windows. There was a gas station a little further down the road with an apartment directly above the pumps. A light went on in one of the windows and I could see a figure peering down at the street.

I turned left onto Warwick Neck Drive at about 9:00pm. The visibility was bad and I could only see a few feet in front of me, so I slowed down to about 20 mph. The road started out paved and smooth, but after a mile or so it narrowed and turned to a bumpy dirt road. Tall oak trees lined either side forming an umbrella over the narrow road, reducing the rain to a mere drizzle. I felt somewhat protected from the storm, and I opened my makeshift window now. I could hear the ocean waves crashing and the smell of salt air. I drove for about a half mile and passed the Aldrich Mansion on my left. The large mansion built by Senator Nelson W. Aldrich in the late 1800's had been in the papers recently. His children had donated the property to the Providence Diocese. I nearly missed a small wooden sign nailed to a tree, which simply read 1030. The paint on the sign had faded away long ago, but you could still make out the address and a long narrow dirt driveway that seemed to disappear into the woods. The sign above it was newly painted and clearly read *no trespassing*.

I decided to turn my lights out, backed up and

turned into the narrow drive. The rain and wind were so loud it would be very difficult for anyone to hear a car engine running outside. I drove down the narrow path for almost a hundred yards, and then noticed that the drive opened to a clearing not far ahead.   I pulled the car into the woods and turned my engine off. In the clearing I could make out the shadowy outline of a small beach house situated on the ocean cliff. The house seemed empty with no signs of life, and there were no lights coming from inside. It was a beach grey bungalow with an unusual widow's walk protruding up from the roofline. The second floor had a large oval window that overlooked the bay.

The spot I had parked my car in was ideal. I had a birds-eye view of the old house, and was far enough off the drive to go undetected by any passerby. I lit up a smoke and I decided to wait and watch for a while. It's amazing how quiet it seems in the middle of a storm. The steady tap of the rain on my car blocked out all other sounds, and gave an impression of total silence from outside. The house seemed quiet, dead, almost abandoned. I watched it for nearly three hours with no signs of life inside before my eyes decided to close around midnight.

I slept for thirty minutes before a loud noise abruptly awoke me. I looked up quickly but saw nothing. The house looked unchanged, quiet and asleep, but the echoing sound in my head had seemed to come from that direction.   I looked back into the woods towards the long entrance drive, and felt confident no one had seen me. I tucked Vincent's gun into my belt as I opened the passenger side door and stepped out leaving the shelter of my vehicle.

I made my way through the woods towards the steep cliff that dropped down into the sea. The forest curved in towards the house so I moved as close as I could without leaving the cover of the trees. When I finally reached the ocean edge, the wind and rain picked up dramatically once I left the protection of the tree line. I was able to make my way down the embankment a few feet, keeping out of anyone's line of site. The cliff consisted of some grass and low brush along the top ridge but turned to mostly rocks after the first several yards. The rocks formed a precipitous slope down to the ocean, which was raging now approximately fifty feet below.

I started along the rocky embankment towards the house, keeping my head below ground level. I tore my pants on some heavy thicket, and held tightly to whatever brush and rocks were available. The gusting wind and rain made a difficult task that much more difficult. I could hear the ocean waves crashing just below me now, but kept my focus on the ground, and slowly made my way towards the back of the house. There was a wooden stairway attached to the cliff that led down to a small dock, which seemed to disappear and reappear with each ocean swell. I ducked under the rail, stepped onto the stairway, and made my way up to a small gate leading into the back yard. I opened the gate, crawled into the yard, and crouched behind an overgrown hedgerow.

The rain wasn't bothering me anymore. I was completely drenched by this point. I waited in silence for several minutes, but heard nothing. I was about twenty feet from the house now, and could easily see the back door and steps leading up to a wrap-a-round porch. Just as I was about to leave the hedge cover, a figure emerged from the back door. I immediately froze. In a moment I heard a match strike, and saw a red glow through the hedgerow. I heard steps pacing on the back porch, and slowly moved my body as low and close to the hedge as I could. I laid there still for nearly five minutes. The rain was pouring down now, and as long as I wasn't spotted, I felt sure he wouldn't leave the shelter of that porch. Finally, I heard steps again and the sound of a door opening and closing.

After a minute, I lifted my head and looked up at the house.   It was as dark and as dead as it had been all night. There were shades drawn on every window, and I couldn't see a dam thing inside.   I could see a small garage in the side yard. So I made my way along the hedgerow, and then crept low over to the side of the garage. The side door was locked, but two of the window panes on it were almost broken. I finished the job, put my hand through and turned the latch, pushing the door open to the left. I hastily entered the garage and closed the door behind me.

There was a musty smell inside, and it took me a few minutes to get my sight in the darkness. I soon made out a black 1939 DeSoto occupying most of the garage. There were no windows on the rolling garage door, just a single paned window on the opposite side wall, with a thick coat of dust making it nearly impossible to see through. I walked in front of the car, and inspected a small wooden workbench. It contained some old paint cans, one bottle of linseed oil, and a small tool box. All of which were covered in dust and cobwebs. No one had used the bench in years. I turned back towards the car, and walked to the passenger side. The car was clean, polished, and clearly well maintained. It was definitely a new visitor to the garage. I opened the passenger side door, and leaned into the vehicle. I pulled out a small pen light that had been given to me by a client who couldn't afford to pay my fee after three weeks of surveillance work. He tried to make up for it by supplying me with a tool of the trade manufactured by his employer. I always kept it on me as a reminder never to take cases on credit again, but occasionally it actually came in handy.

I switched on the light, and pointed it down under the wheel to check the registration. The registration was new, and showed the owner to be a Mr. Arnold Strauss of 210 Blackstone Boulevard, Providence, R.I. I knew the area. The East Side of Providence was pretty well off and populated mostly by mini estates and brownstones. I slipped the card out of its sleeve, and stuffed it into by back pocket. A quick search of the back seat revealed nothing, so I climbed out and popped the trunk open. It contained a spare tire, tire iron, and a case of motor oil. I closed it and walked back towards the garage door.

I gazed out of the broken window pane back towards the house, which still looked lifeless in the dark night. The rain was gusting now, and driving down fiercely on top of the roof. The gutters had fallen long ago, and the heavy rainfall formed a small waterfall off the edge of the roof. Just then I thought I noticed something out of the corner of my eye. I turned my gaze towards the ocean and focused for a moment. After a minute I saw a red light blink twice out on the bay. I couldn't make out its source in the rain and fog, but I put it about a hundred yards offshore. Just then a green light flashed once from a window just below the widows walk. I started to hear the faint sounds of an engine, so I decided to leave the shelter of the garage to get a better look at the shore line below.

I exited the way I had entered, and made my way back towards the cliff line. I kept low and away from the house as I approached the overlook. The wind and rain made it nearly impossible to see anything. I looked over the cliff's edge and drew my attention to the ocean waves breaking violently against the large rocks some fifty feet below.

Just then a small craft appeared out of the fog. You could hear its engine now, which was straining in the heavy seas. The boat looked about 26 feet in length, and a dim light illuminated the small cabin. It slowly approached the rocks below. With each swell the small craft rose and sank ten to fifteen feet. I could hear a faint voice shouting something to someone in the stern, but I couldn't make out was being said. The craft headed for the submerged dock. A ladder protruded out and connected to a cliff stairway leading up into the back yard. Just then a tall lanky man emerged from the cabin and crawled across the bow. He had a rope in one hand, and kept the other hand gripped tightly to the bow rail as he crawled across in the direction of the dock. The driver in the cabin struggled to keep the boat steady, and you could hear the two men shouting profusely at one another. The wind and rain was too loud to make out what they were saying. Just then the tall lanky man tied the rope to a cleat on the bow, shouted one last profanity back at the other man, and jumped onto the submerged dock. He lost his footing for a second as a large swell temporarily submerged him, but held onto the ladder and emerged from the water as the wave withdrew. He tied the other end of the rope to a ladder rung, and began making his way up the ladder to the stairway out of the reach of the crashing waves. Just then I thought I heard a branch snap behind me. I turned back in the direction of the garage and suddenly felt a sharp pain in the back of my head. I fell forward onto the ground as the lights went out

I woke up back in the garage face down on the dirt floor. Half of my face was immersed in sand and grungy motor oil that had been deposited there over the years. The DeSoto was gone now, and someone had apparently dumped me in the garage for safekeeping. Aside from the smell of motor oil on the floor, there was another strong odor that had settled in the garage, which was unusual but I couldn't put my finger on it. As soon as I lifted my head to look around the room began to spin.   My head was throbbing and I could feel a little blood trickling down the back of my neck. I wasn't sure how long I had been out, but since my clothes had dried a little I was guessing it had been for an hour or so. I stood up slowly, grabbed the wall, and asked it to stop moving. After a few minutes it did as I asked, and I was left with a throbbing headache knocking through my brain. I reached at my waist, but Vincent's gun was gone.

I looked over towards the old workbench, and noticed my wallet lying on top. As I walked a little closer I noticed my investigators license had been removed and was lying under a dim florescent lamp hanging over the workbench.   I grabbed both my wallet and the license, and dropped them back in my jacket pocket. The rain was still pouring down hard, and I could hear it pounding on the roof above. Soon heard the sound of two faint voices coming from outside. I staggered back to the window and saw two men who were shouting at each other on the back deck of the house. The old house still seemed lifeless, aside from the two shadowy figures standing out of the rain on the porch. One of the figures was taller and had a lit cigarette. I could see the tip of it gleam red every so often as he took a drag. I heard them arguing with one another, but they were too far away and the rain was coming down too loudly to make out what they were saying. Either way, I didn't care at this point. I had seen enough and already gotten more than I bargained for in one night. I had been sapped pretty badly in the head, and my plan was straightforward now. I needed to get back to my car and go. I tried at the door but it was chained closed from the outside.

Just then I saw the shorter man hand a small object to the taller man. The tall figure tossed his cigarette over the rail and stepped down off the back porch and began making his way across the yard towards the garage. I wasn't sure what they were arguing about or what he had been handed, but it wasn't too hard to imagine what they had in mind for me. I looked quickly around the garage. In the back corner there was a large burlap sack filled with old rags. I grabbed the sack and laid it in the middle of the garage floor in the same spot where I had been placed. I took off my jacket, threw it over the sack, and dropped my hat on top. The light from the workbench was very dim and I thought it might be enough to buy me a few seconds. I hid in the back corner of the garage behind the door. There was an old two by four about three feet in length leaning up against the wall. I grabbed it up and held it high over my head. Just then I heard a key working the padlock on the outside. I heard a chain rattle, and then the brass knob on the side door turned as the door creaked opened towards me.

The sound of the rain and wind outside came gusting in. I held still and waited for him to step completely inside. Now I could see the object he had been handed on the deck. The muzzle of the gun came into view first, and was promptly followed by its owner. He was about five foot ten, a little overweight, maybe 200 pounds. It was dark in the garage, but I could see he was wearing a black long shore man's overcoat with a small knit cap over his head. He took several steps into the garage and was now about three feet from my makeshift dummy. Two shots suddenly rang out and the flash from the muzzle temporarily illuminated the garage. The flash exposed my false decoy in the center of the garage. "Hey, what gives?" he exclaimed as he began to turn around towards me. I moved quickly, slamming the 2 by 4 down on his head. It broke in half. He staggered for a moment and then dropped hard onto the dirt floor. His gun fell from his limp hand onto the ground. I grabbed the revolver and took a few steps back "don't move!" He wasn't moving. The blow had knocked him out cold.   I moved back towards the window and glanced back at the house. The second figure was gone from the back porch now and I couldn't see anyone or anything moving in the house.   I decided it was time to go, so I appropriated the long shore man's overcoat from the thug on the floor. I took off his knit cap, put it on my head, and tucked the revolver away in my waist belt.   I grabbed the pack of smokes from his jacket and lit a cigarette as I opened the door and began casually walking outside.

The wind was really driving hard now, and I was sure if anyone was still watching from the house they would just think it was their man through this heavy rain. I walked slowly around to the back side of the garage smoking my cigarette.   I glanced back at the house, but still no signs of activity.   Once I cornered the garage, I felt I was out of their line of sight and darted into the woods in the direction of my car. I only hoped it was still there and hadn't been discovered.   Two minutes later I had cleared some thicket and spotted my car.   I was in luck. It was still parked where I had left it. I jumped in, started the engine, and peeled out of the woods onto the long driveway with my headlights still off. When I hit the street, I spun the car around, hit the gas pedal and sped back out onto Warwick Neck Drive.

The drive back home was cold and damp, and the steady spray of rain was winning the battle against my make shift window. The downpour was relentless and made it difficult to see more than a few yards ahead. My skull was still screaming at me with each bump in the road. I hit Post Road and headed north. I turned the radio on to get an update on the weather, but only tuned in static. It was a good thirty minutes before I reached the dimly lit driveway of the Garden City Arms Apartments on New London Ave. The Garden City Arms had been my home for the past five years since the owner had hired me to investigate his suspicion that the manager was embezzling money. As it turned it, it was the owner's son, but he decided to dump the manager anyway and I decided to settle in. I pulled into space B22 and turned off the ignition to my car. I barely remember walking though the lobby and taking the elevator to the second floor. My apartment was the third door on the right, which I unlocked and staggered into. I closed the door behind me, and pulled the cord on the brass lamp I kept on my writing desk. My head was banged up good, so I took out a small bottle of aspirin from the desk drawer and swallowed two of the pills. I walked into my bedroom, took my pants off, and fell into bed. Within a minute everything went dark.

5: The Day After

The phone rang at precisely 7:15am the next morning. I had forgotten to take the receiver off the hook before going to sleep, which was my usual practice. My head was definitely unhappy with this oversight. I lifted the receiver "Hello?" I said half asleep. The faint female voice on the other line was muffled. "Is this….. Mr. Chambers…. Mr. Nicholas Chambers?" She spoke in an almost whispered tone. I put the receiver closer to my ear "Could you speak up please, I didn't quite get that." I few seconds passed and then "Is this Nicholas Chambers, the detective?" the voice repeated in an even more muffled tone. I sat up in bed and rubbed my eyes. "Yes it is" I replied. "Who is this calling please?" "I need to speak with you… today if possible?" My head shot up immediately as I broke from my slumber. "Is this Miss. Baxter?" I questioned. The voice became even more muffled to the point where I could barely make out the faint whisper "I'm… I'm not…" and then the line went dead.   "Hello, Hello!" I shouted into the receiver. I lied in bed and waited a while to see if she would call back, but the phone never rang.

I decided to put a call into Detective Bradley of the Providence Police Department. Detective Thomas Bradley and I were old navy buddies. He joined the force as soon as we discharged out, and had made

Detective in less than five years. I went down a different path. "What do you want Chambers?" was the rough greeting I received over the telephone line. "Nice to hear your voice too Tom" I replied. "Look, I got sapped down pretty bad last night. Two thugs with baseball bats caught me in head pretty bad through my driver's side window while I sat in my car. I've got a broken window and an egg on my head to prove it." It wasn't exactly the truth, but I knew the kind of story the cops liked to hear. "So, What do you want from me Chambers?" he replied in an agitated tone. "Look Tom, they dragged me off to some house up by Warwick Neck. I managed to get away, but these fellas meant business if you know what I'm saying. I'm not sure what their racket is, but I thought maybe you could send over a couple of cars and we could take a ride down there to see what gives?"

There was a long pause over the phone, and I could hear a long exasperated sigh on the other end of the line. "Look Nick" he replied. "This isn't your personal body guard service. You always get yourself jammed up and then want us to take a ride with you somewhere. Well that just ain't going happen anymore." he said as his voice grew noticeably more irritated. "If what you say is true, you get your sorry ass down to the station and fill out a report just like any other John Q. Citizen." "But look here Tom…." I tried to interject. He cut me off quickly "and maybe if we buy what you're selling, we'll take a ride out to this place, but without you! Understand?"   "Yeah I get it Tom... loud and clear." I replied as I hung up the telephone while he was still muttering something at me.

An hour later I was dressed and on my way to the Beacon Diner. I thought it might be a good place to start, and besides I hadn't eaten since yesterday afternoon. I knew I needed to put some time in on this missing person case, but she was obviously alive and kicking since she had just called me. Probably didn't want to be found like most missing person's cases. The family always thinks the person has gone missing or been abducted, but nine out of ten times with these cases you end up finding the person hidden away in some corner of the world on their own accord. My mind kept going back to last night and that bungalow on the cliff. What was the Palaeno doing waiting in my car, and who was he working for? More importantly, what was going on at that house?

I pulled up to the Beacon Diner at 8:35am. The parking lot was nearly empty, aside from an old rusted out Ford pickup and a blue Chevrolet sedan with a broken tail light parked in front. The weather was cloudy now and getting pretty overcast. It looked like the rain had subsided for the time being, but wasn't quite finished with us yet. I jumped a large puddle in front of the diner and ascended three rusty metal stairs. A small bell rang as I entered through a screen door at the front of the diner. There was an elderly man in his seventies parked at the counter eating some burnt toast and eggs and drinking black coffee from a dirty cup. I turned to notice a young mother and a small child in one of the booths at the opposite end of the diner. She was yelling at him and wiping jelly off his face.

I walked up to the far end of the counter and planted myself on one of the stools. Jo Stafford was playing in the background on an old juke box. Just then a young woman, maybe in her early twenties, emerged from the back kitchen. She had short blond hair with bangs just above her eyes, and a pencil tucked behind her right ear. She wore a powder blue jump skirt with a white button up cotton blouse. The name Evelyn was embroidered on the left pocket, which also held a small writing pad. She approached the old man and asked if he needed more coffee. He muttered something incoherently and she reached over, grabbed the pot of coffee, and refilled his cup. He grunted a thank you to her without looking up.

She walked over to my section of the counter with pot in hand "coffee mister?" "Thanks" I nodded in approval. She turned my cup over and filled it, and dropped two sugar cubes on the side of the saucer. "Cream is in the carafe if you need it. Do you want a menu?" "No" I replied. "I'll just have two eggs and some toast please."

"How do you want your eggs?" she asked. "Once over please… and I take the morning paper if you have it." I replied. She nodded and walked off.

The Beacon Diner looked like it was probably built in the early twenties. The counters and cabinets looked original and had an older art deco feel to them. The record on the juke box was changing over now, and horns from the Glen Miller Band began to sound out. One of the speakers must have blown because there was a scratchy sound tarnishing the music. There were frosted doubled paned windows at each of the booths, with dusty flowered curtains pulled back on each side.

Five minutes later the waitress reappeared from the kitchen with my eggs and toast in hand. "Here you go mister, how's the coffee holding out?" she asked as she placed my breakfast down on the counter top.   "I'll have a refill and maybe a little conversation if you're up to it" I replied. She reached for the coffee pot on the back counter and poured me another cup. "Pretty quiet morning" I said while dropping two more sugar cubes into my coffee. "You said it mister. This dam rain is keeping everyone at home I guess." She replied. "We almost didn't open this morning, but my cheapskate boss didn't want to lose a day's receipts."

I pulled the sister's photo out of my pocket and slid it across the countertop in front of her as I began eating my toast. "Have you seen this girl around lately?" I questioned. She glanced down at the photo, lifted her head back up a little and asked "Police?"
"No. My name's Nicholas Chambers, I'm a private investigator. Her family hired me to find her. They haven't heard from her in some time and are starting to get worried" I replied. "Wow, a shamus! Like in the pictures?" she asked. "Yeah, just like in the pictures" I rolled my eyes. "But her family is getting pretty worried." She turned her back to me and returned the coffee pot to its base. She paused for a moment, spun around and gave me the once over, trying to decide if I was playing it straight or not. She finally leaned over and put her two elbows on the countertop "She's a regular. Usually comes in with her boyfriend. Seems like a good kid, although I'm not so sure about the boyfriend." "Why?" I asked. She leaned down closer to me where only I could hear what she was saying "A little too well dressed for my liking, if you know what I mean? Usually meets her here every Tuesday. He's a good tipper... but I really couldn't see the two of them together. She seemed so innocent and he just makes my skin crawl." She stood up again and I threw another question at her "Have they been by lately?" "No" she replied. "I

haven't seen either of them in a couple of weeks." "Well thanks anyway" I said as I dropped my card on the counter. "If she does come in, would you mind dropping me a line? I'd be grateful." "Sure thing!" She picked up my card, tucked it in her blouse, smiled and walked away.

I finished my breakfast and paid my check. As I walked out the Diner, I noticed the rain had started up again. I could hear bursts of thunder rumbling in the distance. The clouds looked dark and ominous. As I stepped down off the rusty entrance steps I noticed a dark green Chevrolet coupe parked one block down. It suddenly started its engine and drove off. As it sped by me, I couldn't make out the driver other than to see she was definitely female. I glanced quickly at the rear plate. *KPY was* all I could make out. I thought for a moment about following the car, but decided there was probably nothing to it. I needed to get down to the Journal building and check in with Allison's boss.

The Providence Journal was located downtown at 75 Fountain Street near the train station. Over the years, my work had brought me to the Journal from time to time on behalf of clients. During my last visit, one of the editors felt the need to have me abruptly escorted out of the building by security. Since then, the guards seemed a little less hospitable towards me whenever I visited. Since it was Saturday morning, the security guards would not be working down in the front lobby as they always did during the week. I parked my car about a block away and walked across the rain drenched street to the building's front entrance. Looming clouds darkened the sky, but the rain had subsided for the moment.

The main entrance to the Journal Building had an unimpressive set of worn granite steps leading up to two large doors made of thick tinted glass with tarnished brass trim. The words "The Providence Journal / The Evening Bulletin" were embossed in gold leaf on one of the doors. There was a large sign in the lower right hand corner of the door stating "No Solicitation". I ignored the sign and walked inside.

The main lobby floor was constructed of beige and white Italian marble.   A young man in his early twenties worked a mop in the far corner of the lobby polishing the floor to impress visitors like myself.   Large antique white paper drapes with an art deco pattern lined the tall windows facing Fountain St.   In the center of the lobby was a large semi-circular reception desk with a slate black countertop that reminded me of the bridge on my old ship. Seated at the center of the bridge was a peculiar looking man in his sixties, with large brown spectacles. He looked as if he had been seated at the bridge all his life.   He wore a gray tattered flannel shirt with a soiled coffee-stained brown tie. What was left of his receding gray hair was sculpted back over an expanding bald spot on the top of his head. Across from the Lobby desk were two brass-faced elevators numbered one and two.

"Ahoy Captain" I said as I approached the lobby desk. "What's that?" the man uttered as he drew his attention up from the crossword he had been working on.   "Names Tim Baxter", I said as I leaned up against the reception counter. "I just drove up from New York to visit my sister Allison who works upstairs in Research."   "Sign the visitor's book please" he replied as he stood up slowly from his seat and handed me a pencil. He started to fumble through some worn out pages of an old worn out book.   I took the pencil and signed in as Tim Baxter, visiting one Allison Baxter in the Research Department.   I handed his pencil back to him as he looked up and pointed me to the two elevators directly across from the bridge. "Take the elevator to the fourth floor please, and ring the bell outside of the Research Office, that's 4C. Someone will help you up there" he said in a very authoritative tone. I thanked him and walked over to the elevators on the other side of the lobby. Each of the brass doors was framed in a neoclassical design of elegant mahogany, which didn't seem to fit the rest of the lobby décor. I pushed the up button and within a minute the elevator door rolled open. I hopped onboard and pushed number four.

The fourth floor was dull, dreary, and darkened with shaded windows on either end of the hallway. The floor had gray painted walls with green trim around each doorway. Tan file cabinets lined one side of the corridor, each stacked high with stale brown storage boxes. Frosted plate glass doors numbered 4A through 4J alternated on each side of the floor. I walked to the right of the elevators and found 4C. There was a small buzzer outside of the door with a hand written note stating *please ring bell* posted just below it.

I knocked on the plate glass three times and waited. No one responded. I knocked three more times, making sure to let my ring connect sufficiently with the window glass. I heard a shuffle of footsteps from inside the office and the sound of someone approaching now. It was definitely a woman's high heels clicking their way closer to the door. Just then a shadow appeared through the frosted plate glass. The tarnished brass doorknob turned and the door creaked opened slowly about a foot. A small middle-aged woman poked her head out of from door just far enough for me to see the disapproving look on her face. "Don't read much do you!" she snapped in a school teacher's tone, while pointing over at the make-shift sign. "Oh… I must have missed that, sorry." I replied. "Good Morning Miss, my name is Tim Baxter, Allison's brother. I'm looking for the head of the Research Department. Would he be in today?" I inquired. She was a thin woman with a beak nose and long brown hair that was graying on the sides and pulled back into a pony tail. She wore green tinted glasses with a gold frame and silver design along the top. She looked to be in her fifties, and was all business from head to toe. She reminded me of my 6th grade English teacher. "Wait here please!" she replied as she abruptly slammed the door in my face.

I could hear her footsteps as she walked away on the opposite side of the door.   The smell of ink permeated the hallway, and it reminded me of my first summer job at the Coventry Town Library. A few moments passed and the footsteps returned. The door knob clicked open again and the door swung out. "Follow me!" she said in an annoyed tone as she turned and walked back inside of the office. As I entered the room I noticed it was quite large and spacious, with lofty twenty foot ceilings. Several rows of unoccupied desks with typewriters lined the room from side to side, and approximately twenty shaded lamps hung from the ceiling above them. There were four office doors on the opposite side of the room, and only one was presently open with the lights on inside. That seemed to be where we were headed. As she approached the open door she knocked on the outer frame "Mr. Baxter here to see you Mr. Thompson" she said while gesturing for me to enter the office. "Thanks" I replied as I strolled into the office.

Mr. Thompson was short, about five feet six inches tall, and maybe a just shy of a hundred and fifty pounds. He was wearing a dark tweed sports jacket and a dirty wrinkled lilac shirt with a navy blue bow tie that was drooping down on one side. He had thinning brown hair and wore round marbleized black rimmed spectacles. I noticed a large scar on the left side of his throat that seemed out of place, and there was black stitching on the pocket of his shirt with the initials E.T.

He looked up as I entered the room. "Good morning Mr. Baxter, I'm Allison's Manager Edward Thompson. I'm quite busy at the moment, so what can I do for you?" he offered as he reached his hand out to me. "Good morning Mr. Thompson" I replied. "Nicholas Chambers, Private Investigator" He stood up suddenly "now wait just a minute! Who let you in here?" he exclaimed while becoming extremely disjointed. "I've been hired by Allison's family to find her" I replied. He sat back down slowly, shot me a nasty glance, and gestured for me to sit in one of the two oak chairs opposite his boring desk. Both chairs were pushed tightly up against the desk, which gave me the impression he didn't have visitors to his office very often. "Well what can I do for you Mr. Chambers?" he asked.

I took a quick glance around. His office was dull and drab with nothing remarkable to comment on. No family pictures, no plaques or the customary awards you might typically see in an executive's office. Stacks of papers lined his desk and filled a side credenza. Each had a smaller piece of paper with notes on it attached with paper clips. His desk was made of plain gray metal with a green Formica top, similar to the ones we had used in the military. "Well Mr. Thompson..." I said as I removed my hat and looked back at him. "Allison has been missing for nearly three weeks. The family is getting worried and I was wondering if you might have some idea where she is? Maybe sent on an assignment out-of-state or something of that sort?" I asked. He glanced down at his desk for a moment, peering at a gold pen which he picked up and began twirling with his fingertips. "No... no idea whatsoever... The sister came by here earlier in the week asking me the same questions. Unfortunately,

I don't think I can be much help to you. Allison hasn't shown up for work at all during the past two weeks. I tried to reach her by telephone at her apartment, but wasn't able to get a hold of her. To be honest, it's gotten to the point that her position here at the Journal is compromised unless she comes in soon and explains herself." he said with some measure of annoyance.

"Well, there must have been something?" I replied. "Was she assigned to any special case? What type of research was she involved with? It may have had something to do with her disappearance." He looked up at me with a frustrated expression on his face, which had begun to turn a light shade of red by this point. "Look here…" he replied slowly, "There is nothing I can tell you other then she has not been here for the past two weeks, and she is mostly likely headed for the unemployment line! She did mundane research on the stock market, corporate filings, and had just started a project on fish migration in Narragansett Bay. There was nothing remarkable in the least!" He went on "If you ask me she just got involved with the wrong crowd when she began dating that hoodlum character" he exclaimed. His tone changed a little "Please understand that I am very fond of Allison, and she did a nice job for us, but I can't continue on for much longer without replacing her position. So if you do find her, let her know she needs to contact me immediately." He stood up from his desk giving me the signal our time together was over. "Now I must insist you leave me to my work Mr. Chambers, or do I need to ring for security?"

"That won't be necessary" I replied as I stood up from my seat. "Thank you for your time Mr. Thompson. I'll find my way out. If you do hear from Allison please contact me so I can let her family know she's ok." I dropped my card on his desk and began to exit his office. I turned around in the doorway and threw one last question at him "not from this area are you Mr. Thompson? I'm picking up a very slight accent in your voice, maybe Pennsylvania?" He looked up at me and shook his head "you're detective skills must be a little off today Mr. Chambers. Born and raised in Providence. I've lived here all my life." Maybe... I thought to myself as I nodded and walked out.

I walked back through the large spacious room with rows of vacant desks and typewriters. I saw the English teacher seated at a small desk in a far corner of the room, pounding away rapidly on the keys of a Smith Corona typewriter. She paused to shoot me a contempt filled glance and quickly returned to banging away on her keys. As I exited the outer office door I glanced back at Thompson's Office. He was still standing by his desk with the door slightly open, but was now speaking on the telephone.

The Providence Police station was only two blocks away from the Journal building. I decided to leave my car parked and pay a visit to my friend Detective Bradley. The wind and rain had picked up again and was driving hard against the black city streets. The smell of salt water from the bay permeated the city now, as I turned up the collar on my overcoat and let the wind blow me down Fountain Street towards Empire.

The Providence Police Station was a large white granite four story building, which had been built in the 1920's. Detective Bradley had a small office on the second floor and was assigned to the homicide division. I entered the building through a small stainless steel door on the side of the building in an attempt to avoid the desk Sergeant who was usually posted in the main lobby. I walked into a narrow hallway on the first floor and shook off like a wet dog. The white tiled floor was puddled up with street water that had been dragged in by other wet dogs like me. I took off my soaked hat and overcoat and hung them both up on a set of hangers along the back wall. There was a musty smell permeating through the hallway. It was that old dingy building smell that you always find in stuffy police stations. Three officers dressed in dark blue uniforms were speaking intensely at the far end of the hallway, while another detective had a thin scrawny man handcuffed waiting by the elevators. A well dressed young woman in her twenties was seated in a waiting area outside of a small double paned reception window. She was reading the daily paper and only gave me a passing glance as I walked by. I saw a doorway to the stairway just to the left of me, which I immediately headed for. The elevators at the station had a bad reputation for breaking down. I had gotten stuck once myself for nearly three hours with a very talkative elderly gentleman one hot day last summer. Since then I always made a point to take the stairway.

I climbed the first set of stairs and opened the door to the second floor. The floor was noticeably louder, and I heard dozens of people talking with the sound of typewriters banging away in the background. I could make out at least six separate conversations going on in the offices strung along the corridor. In one office a detective was questioning a large scruffy shirtless man who was handcuffed to a bar on the side of his desk. As I passed the next room, I noticed a young woman who was balling her eyes out, and muttering something about not stealing a dress from Shepards. At that moment an older man in his forties emerged from one of the offices grasping at the ear of a young boy in his teens who appeared to be his son. "Wait till I get home to your mother!" was all I could make out as they rushed by. I approached Tom's office and knocked several times on a closed door. I heard a faint "come in" respond from inside, so I opened the door and strolled inside.

"Hey Pal, how's tricks?" I asked as I sat down in a small wooden chair positioned aside of his diminutive desk. His office was all of 50 square feet, and his desk was pushed flush up against one wall with his side facing the doorway.

His desktop was home to a single pad of plain white paper, a typewriter, and an old tin mug with two broken pencils in it. Detective Bradley was about 6'2" in height, and weighed approximately 210 pounds. He had short straight brown hair parted off to the side. He was happily married to his wife Marsha for the past fifteen years, and had two daughters in grammar school. He had just turned forty-three two weeks ago. I knew this because a mutual friend had told me about the birthday party Tom had forgotten to invite me to.

Ignoring my greeting, he turned his attention slowly away from the report in front of him, removed his reading glasses and looked up at me. "What type of case are you working on Chambers?" "It's nice to see you too Tom. It's been a while." I replied. "Well, nothing too exciting, just a missing person case." "Tell me a little more about it." he questioned. I looked up at him with a skeptical expression "There's not that much to tell. The girl went missing about two weeks ago, and the family is starting to get nervous. Her sister came in last night and hired me to find her. Why the sudden interest Tom?" I asked. He smiled and glanced back up at me "You know I'm always interested in your work, any leads yet?" he asked a little too casually. "Nothing but dead ends so far" I replied. "Girl had a boyfriend the family wasn't crazy about. My money is she ran off to get married on the down low." He just nodded his head without responding.

"Look that's not why I'm here Tom. I need to talk to you about what happened to me last night." I reached over and grabbed the pencil and paper pad on his desk. I jotted down the address of the house on Warwick Neck. "Like I said on the phone, I got sapped pretty bad last night, and the crew that did it was camped out at this address down near the water in Warwick. I'm not sure what their racket is, but I can tell you they meant business." He turned away from me and looked out of a partially shaded window that faced a back alley behind the station. "You would think after ten years of service they would give me a little nicer office, with a better view of the city... I'm third man in line from a seniority standpoint, but I still have the worst office in the Detective Division. You know why that is Chambers?" he asked. "Maybe they just don't like your quirky sense of humor?" I jokingly replied. He wasn't laughing "Maybe they just don't like the company I keep, you ever think of that?" "No pretty sure it's your quirky sense of humor" I replied.

He turned back towards me and sat down in his seat. "You'll need to fill out a report, and then we can check into it. But before we go down that road, how about you take a walk with me downstairs, and we pay a little visit to the morgue?" he suggested. "Found a dead girl down at the shipyard early this morning, could be your missing person?" My head jolted up "What time was she found?" I asked. He scratched his head for a moment and then replied "Just around 7:00am I think. Why?" A small sense of relief came over me "Well, I forgot to mention that my missing person called me this morning around the same time. So I doubt if it's my girl" I replied. He shrugged his shoulders and nodded "Well, why don't you take a walk with me just the same. Especially since this girl had your card stashed away in her wallet." I didn't say anything for a moment, and then replied "Let's go!"

The city morgue was located in a building just adjacent to the police station, but department personnel could get to it through a tunnel located in their basement. Detective Bradley brought me down using the same elevator I had spent several hours residing in last summer. This time it did its job. We walked out of the elevator into the dingy dimly lit basement hallway of the Providence Police Department. The basement floor was made of old busted up green asbestos tiles, and there were several storage rooms on either side with padlocks on each door. A blue light was lit above a door towards the far end of the hallway. As we approached the locked door I noticed some lettering on it that read *213 Empire Street, City Morgue, Authorized Personnel Only!* Tom pulled a set of keys from his pocket and unlocked the door. That led us into a short tunnel with a dirt floor. It had a low brick ceiling that was no more than seven feet in height, and was dripping water at the moment. On the opposite side of the tunnel was another door with another lock that we passed through to enter into the city morgue.

As we entered, the smell of formaldehyde and burning blood immediately hit me. It was the kind of odor you know will stick to your cloths once you leave the building. The police basement entrance led right into the main autopsy room. There was a large stainless steel double door on the opposite side of the room that led to a walk-in refrigerator where the residents were stored. At the moment, the autopsy room had two occupants lying on examination tables. One was covered and the second was a young man still tangled in what appeared to be ropes and fishing net. The smell of seaweed and fish began to block out the formaldehyde odor. "What happened to him" I questioned as we walked by the body. Tom looked back quickly and replied "washed up on Warwick Point Beach this morning. A couple of locals found him and called it in. The wagon just brought him down. Some type of fishing accident, twenty year old lobsterman out of Oakland Beach. Out pulling pots last night if you can believe that." I took a good look at the young man as I passed by. He had curly dirty blonde hair that was covered in beach sand and what appeared to be dried blood dripping down his face.   His eyes were still wide open, and skin and lips were a cool shade of purple. He wore a St. Christopher medal around his neck on a rope necklace. Tom walked to the other side of the room and removed his overcoat.

"Here's your girl Chambers" he said as he approached the second body, which was still covered in a white sheet.   He lifted the sheet and revealed the face of a young woman underneath. "What about it? Is this your missing girl?" I looked at her raven black hair and the bluish face that was so attractive just hours earlier. Now a dark brown substance was caked along one side of her face. She was still wearing the same red blouse and tight black skirt, but they were both coated in dried mud now. "No", I replied with a short pause "...... She was my client". He turned and looked down at her. "Not anymore."   He turned her head to one side and revealed two small holes in her temple, each the size of my pinky with dried blood oozing out. "What do you make of these chambers?" he asked while pointing his index finger at the two bullet holes. I looked her over good one last time and replied "Well, someone wanted her dead, and it looks like they got what they wanted." A frustrated expression came over his tired face as he shot back at me "That's brilliant detective work Nick. You learn that in P.I. school? Two 9mm slugs point blank to the side of the head, and her hands were tied with rope behind her back. One of the yard workers found her down in the shipyard lying behind warehouse number nineteen. What was her name?" I shook my head and replied "Jill Baxter, her sister Allison went missing a couple of weeks ago. I don't know much more then that Tom."

Did they find any shell casings at the scene?" I questioned. He covered her face again with the sheet and replied "No… the boys swept the area, but came up empty. Any leads on her sister? Don't hold back on me with this one Nick, your card was tucked away in her blouse pocket. I was just about to issue an APB on you, when you strolled into my office." I shrugged my shoulders and looked over at him "I just met her last night. She paid me a c-note in advance to find her sister. Gave me a couple of leads, but both were dead ends. It's obviously more than just a missing person's case, but that's all I have right now Tom.... good enough?" I asked. He started to put his overcoat back on "It's definitely not good enough, but it will have to do for now. Be sure to keep me in the loop on this Nick, or I won't be able to help you much." It was about that time

that I felt a sudden urge to get on with my day.
"Ok, well I think I be on my way Tom.   The sooner I get moving, the sooner I can dig into this" I offered.
"What about your assault report" he questioned.   "It can wait" I replied. Fifteen minutes later I was back in my car heading off to the Providence Shipyard.

The Providence Shipyard was located just south of the city along Allens Avenue. It was host to dozens of warehouses that stored freight and materials being unloaded onto seven major docks along a two mile stretch of Narragansett Bay. Railroad tracks ran throughout the shipyard, allowing banging freight trains easy access to cargo they would carry to distant destinations throughout the country. One of those trains was pulling out as I approached the main entrance to the Shipyard. A black and white checkered gate lowered itself and a red signal light began flashing. A loud warning bell started ringing as the train approached. I stopped at the crossing just as the locomotive lumbered slowly across the road pulling two dozen coal filled cars in its wake. I could make out the shadow of a conductor through the filthy window of the locomotive engine. As more cars passed I noticed two hobos sitting on the rear end of one of them with their legs hanging over the back tail gate. One was whittling on a stick with a pocket knife, while the second appeared to somehow be sleeping. They both looked to be in need of a shave and a fresh set of cloths. The loud clanging of the passing train along with the ringing from the overhead bell was more than my aching head could handle at this point. It took a good five minutes, but the slow moving train finally passed by allowing the noise to dissipate. The gates rose upright again and I hit my gas pedal.

I drove on down into the shipyard along Terminal Street, passing several large tankers that were tied up at one of the main piers. The first ship I passed was from Venezuela and was unloading crates of coffee into three trucks parked alongside the ship on the pier. Tired wet men worked the ropes and pulleys shouting to each other as the large barrels made their way dockside. A second rusted out ship with the name *Argentine Mist* printed on its bow sat quietly, aside from a few lights burning in its bridge. One man in a yellow rain coat stood on the bow in the pouring rain smoking a cigarette and overlooking the docks.

It was still coming down pretty heavy as I pulled my car into the parking lot of warehouse nineteen. The warehouse looked like any other building along Terminal Street. It had red brick construction with large multi-pane windows lining all sides on two floors. A large smoke stack towards the rear of the building was spewing black fumes out into the gray clouded sky. The front of the building had two large neglected garage doors and one side entrance door, all of which were closed at the moment. I drove around to the back of the building where Tom had said her body had been found. I parked right up against the back brick wall, and put my hat and trench coat back on. I pulled out a cigarette, lit it up and stepped out into the wind and rain.

I took a good look around. It was a good spot. A line of trees blocked the view from the main road, while two large water towers and an electrical transmission tower completely blocked the line of sight from the other side of the shipyard. It was totally isolated with no lights in the rear of the building. Definitely a good place to dump a body! I took a quick look at the dirt covered ground but couldn't see anything out of the ordinary. Tom said they hadn't found any shell casings, but last night's heavy rain could have easily washed them away or buried them in the mud by now. I decided to take a walk around to the front of the building. As I rounded the corner to the side of the warehouse, I felt the heavy wind and rain gusting off of Narragansett Bay hit my face. The storm had awoken from its earlier lull and was back in full stride. I walked out to the front of the building and looked across the street out onto the bay. The swells out on the ocean had to be fifteen feet now, and the only ships in sight were those tied securely to the shipyard piers. The gray sky was overcast and filled with darkened black clouds, which seemed to be moving along at a good clip overhead.

Just then I heard the rattle of a garage door opening up behind me. I turned to see three men emerge from the warehouse. One was a large overweight stout character with blue jeans and a leather vest jacket. He had brownish gray curly hair and a bald spot that was taking up most of his head. He had an unlit cigar clinging to the side of mouth, and a broken pencil tucked over his right ear. He held a clipboard in his left hand and was barking at two younger workers who just nodded their heads in fear. "Just get that truck loaded by 2:00pm or it's both of your asses. Got it!" he shouted. I assumed he was the foreman. The two younger men just nodded their heads, put their tails between their legs, and ran off aimlessly into the rain.

He turned his attention towards me now. "I thought you detectives finished up here already?" he questioned. I took one last drag and threw my but to the ground. "Just had a few more questions..." I replied as I approached him. "Was anyone in the building last night at all?" I asked. He shot an irritated look back at me and replied "Look… I already told the other detective that the whistle blows at 5pm and this place turns into a ghost town. I locked the place up myself at 5:45pm. I came in this morning to open up around 7:00am and everything seemed fine." I scratched my head as detectives tend to do "… and what time did you find the girl?" I asked. He looked back at me "Sent one of the young guys out back around 8:00am to empty the trash. He walked out the back door and saw her lying there, then screamed for help and a few of us went running out. To be honest, it kind of freaked us all out. There she was lying face up in the mud, hands tied behind her back, and her eyes were still wide open.   Well, that's when we rang you guys up." I nodded my head and probed a little further "So nobody saw the body there when you first came in?" He pulled a lighter out of his pocket and lit up his half smoked cigar.   A few puffs later he replied "Like I said earlier, all my guys either come in on the bus or park on the side of the building where the pavement is.   Nobody parks in the back, so we wouldn't have noticed one way or the other."

Just then a large wave crashed against the stone sea wall across the street.   The heavy wind gusts carried the salt water across the road and lacquered us up pretty good.   The foreman was getting impatient now "I need to get back inside now..." I held my hand up "Just one last question. Did you notice any unusual activities going on around the shipyard lately, anything out of the ordinary?" I inquired. He blew a little air out of his mouth "No nothing, same old same ole around here" he replied as he turned and headed back for the garage.   He took a few steps and then turned back towards me asking "Hey Detective, you never showed me your badge, aren't you guys suppose to do that?" he questioned. "You never asked to see it" I responded as I headed back in the direction of my car. He stared back at me in a not so friendly way "Never got your name either mister?" he shouted. I stopped and turned back to look at him "Nick Chambers,

Private Investigator" I replied in a very calm voice. He shook his head and threw his clipboard down on the ground. "Get the hell out of here shamus, before someone helps you on your way! We don't like people poking around where they don't belong!" he shouted.

"Especially dead women?" I questioned. He just shook his head in disgust, flicked his cigar at me and walked back into the garage. Within a few seconds I heard the rusty garage door rolling back down and finally slamming shut. The handle in the middle of the door turned horizontally and I heard the locking mechanism click into place. I had worn out my welcome as I sometimes did. I slithered back into my car, and headed home.

It took me about thirty minutes to make my way back home, and it was just about 5:00pm when I pulled into 2300 New London Ave. It had been a long day and I was nowhere with a dead client. I was still trying to put everything together in my head as I pulled a few bills out from my postal box in the main lobby. I took the stairs up to the second floor and was still reading my mail as I unlocked the door and walked into my apartment. As soon as I entered I caught the faint smell of moth balls and cheap cologne lingering in the air. I had the feeling I was not alone in the room. I turned quickly to look behind the open door but it was too late. I felt a sudden sharp pain invade the top of my head as my knees buckled and fell to the floor. Everything went Dark once again.

I woke up in a small living room. As I opened my eyes, the room looked blurry and my head was still spinning. Vague shapes soon began to take form. The lighting was dim, and I was lying on a blue silk sofa with gold harps printed in the fabric. There was a red and gold oriental rug at the center of the room, and a slate tile fireplace stood directly across from me with a white marble mantle above it. There was a statue of the Virgin Mary on the mantel along with a picture of Christ gazing up towards the sky. A large intimidating man sat in an easy chair at the

far corner of the room. He wore a tan trench coat
and his hat sat silently on his lap. His right hand
was placed hidden under the hat, and I could make
out the glimmer of a gun muzzle protruding from
underneath. I could smell spaghetti sauce cooking,
and fresh bread baking nearby. I lifted my head and
the room decided to spin a little more, so I put it
back where it was. I could hear the rain still
pounding on the window outside.

Just then the man seated in the corner stood up
"He's waking up boss" he shouted as he moved
closer to me. "Molto bene! Just in time for dinner" I
heard another voice reply in the background. The
man walked beside me and slapped me upside the
head with his left hand. "Get up" he exclaimed.
Now I could clearly see the revolver in his right
hand pointed at my chest. "Sure thing" I said as I
slowly sat up in couch. My head started to ring,
and the room seemed to be rotating even more as I
sat up. The man grabbed my elbow and helped me
up off the couch, while he jammed the barrel of the
revolver into my ribs. He walked me around the
corner of the living room into a small dining room.
The room was painted light blue, with a white
wainscoting along the lower section of the wall.
The table had a white lace table cloth and was set
with two place settings. A gallon of red wine was
sitting in the center of the table, and freshly baked
bread was placed on a chopping block with butter
and olive oil on the side. There was a large salad

bowl in the center of the table, and a large bowl of cooked spaghetti. The man with the gun sat me down at the far end of the table, and sat himself in the corner behind me, and out of my view.

Just then a tall rugged looking olive skinned man entered the room holding a large pan of sauce containing meatballs and sausage. He was holding the pan with two oven mitts, and laid it down on the table on top of an old kitchen towel. I recognized the man from the newspapers as Johnny Corrao. He looked to be in his early forties with jet black wavy hair and broad shoulders. He was dressed in a pair of black slacks and a white silk button up shirt with his initials embroidered on the cuffs and pocket. His shirt was unbuttoned at the top and a gold chain with a crucifix attached was hanging around his neck. A shinny gold watch wrapped itself around his wrist, and he wore two silver cufflinks on each of his sleeves. The papers had recently reported his release from the state pen after an eighteen month stint for racketeering.

He was the son of big Tony Corrao, who was gunned down two years earlier in front of his own coffee shop on Federal Hill. Johnny was the heir apparent, and had taken over the family businesses. The two punks who had gunned his father down were found dead down by the Providence River two weeks later. They each had over twenty gunshots in them, and their heads had been beaten in with baseball bats to ensure they would need closed casket funerals. One thing I knew for sure was that these guys meant business.

He sat down opposite me at the table and spoke up "Come stai Chambers? Sono il pane." He pulled out a large carving knife and began cutting up the bread. He poured some olive oil on a small plate along with the bread and passed it to me. "Per favore, mangiate!" he said. "You'll feel better". I took the bread and began to nibble on it without responding. It had been a long day and I was getting a little hungry anyway. He looked me over as he helped himself to some spaghetti. He poured some sauce over it, and added two meatballs to his plate. "Nobody takes the time to make gravy right anymore. Everyone's in a rush these days. You know what I'm saying Chambers?" "I guess so" I replied. He looked up at me as he began eating "I'm not sure you do, that's why I wanted to speak with you" he quipped. "You're lucky Chambers. Joey just wanted to plug you and throw you in the river. I told him we needed to talk first." The sauce smelled pretty good, and the room had started to stabilize, so I helped myself to a plate and spoke up "What can I do for you Mr. Corrao?" I had learned that these mob guys liked to be called Mister. Call them by their first name, and they'd smash your face in.

He finished chewing a meatball and poured himself

a full glass of red wine, which looked to be of the homemade brand. He wiped his mouth with a cloth napkin "Any leads on Allison yet?"   I glanced around the room quickly. It seemed like Corrao and the gunsel were the only other two people in the apartment. I was actually wondering why he had the gunsel. He was safe with or without a gun in the room. I kept thinking back to the old man who was the accountant for his dad. This guy was in his late eighties, and he would walk up federal hill to the bank each morning with a wheel barrel full of cash they had taken in at the club the night before. Nobody ever touched him. Everyone knew who he was and what the consequences would be if you touched him.   I looked back towards Johnny "I'd like to talk to you, but I'm not sure what you mean?" He laughed and motioned to the gunman "Joey, andare a prendere l'incudine!" he said while calmly sipping on his wine glass. "I know you've been poking around, so just tell me what you found out" he asked very directly.

Just then the gunman walked back into the room with a large muscular man in his fifties who was carrying a fifty pound iron anvil and a few yards of rope. The gunsel stood behind me and held his revolver to the back of my head as the second man began tying my wrist to the top of the anvil. The gunman whispered a few words in my ear. "Hold still Chambers or I'll have to blow your friggin head off." I looked down at the anvil my left hand was being secured to and noticed what seemed to be dried blood and pieces of skin still stuck to it. "Hey guys, I think we may have gotten off on the wrong foot here…" Just then the older man opened the drawer of the corner china cabinet and pulled out a small sledge hammer. I didn't like where this was heading. Corrao looked over at me as he wiped the sauce off of his face with a napkin. "I was hoping we could be gentleman about this Chambers, but it's always the hard way with you PI's. Last chance to tell me what you know?" The large man approached my side with the sledge hammer in his hand, and I could still feel the cool muzzle of Joey's gun pushing up against the back of my neck. I felt a drop of sweat roll down the side of my face. "Ok Guys, I can see you're not much for small talk. No need to get all worked up. I may have some ideas."

Corrao stood up and gave a little chuckle. He walked over to the china cabinet to retrieve another wine glass. "E divertende, you're alright Chambers" he said as he motioned to the older man to hold off. He pulled up the chair directly across from me, sat down, and filled the second glass with wine from the unlabeled bottle "Bevi, so start talking". "I talk a little better with my hands free?" I asked looking down at my left side. Corrao looked across the table at me "I think we'll leave that as is for now, just to keep you honest. Right Anthony?" he asked the large man standing over me who was still holding the small sledge. "Si" was all the man replied.

I rubbed my neck with my right hand and started talking "The sister hired me last night to find Allison. I'm just one day into this thing, so there's really not a whole lot to go on at this point." That didn't seem to satisfy Corrao, so I moved on. "I stopped by the Beacon Diner this morning and nobody has seen her there for some time. The last time was with you a couple of weeks ago. So I decided to take a drive by the Journal to talk with her boss, but she hasn't been to work for almost two weeks. He mentioned something about her losing her job." Corrao cut in "I'll take care of that… Go on" he said. I went on "Well, it was about that time that I found out my client was dead."

Corrao pulled back in his seat, it startled him. "Cio che, what did you just say?" he questioned. "My client, the sister, dead!" I replied. He stood up out his chair and began pacing across the room "You sure about this Chambers?" I shook my head and replied "Unless she just likes passing time on weekends lying on a stainless steel table down at the City Morgue? Yeah she's dead alright, found early this morning down by the shipyard with two slugs in her head." Corrao pulled the large man off to the side and whispered something in his ear. The man nodded and left the room, leaving the sledge on the side board. He turned back towards me.

"What else?" "After that, I took a ride down to the shipyard to see what I could see. Spoke with the foreman at the warehouse where she was found. It sounds like it was pretty deserted there last night. There was nobody working around the place, so no witnesses. Police aren't sure if she was shot there or shot somewhere else and just dumped there. Good spot for it either way." I paused for a moment and then continued "Well, that's about it, up until you're man sapped me down and brought me here. So far just a lot of dead ends."

He stood for a moment in deep thought rubbing the back of his neck, and then decided to sit back down. He poured himself another glass of vino, took a few sips without saying anything, and then spoke up. "Her name was Charlotte. She worked as a dancer for me downstairs at the club on weekends. Nice kid, we actually dated for a while." He didn't look up at me, just kept staring at the tablecloth. "She wanted to be an actor and needed some extra dough, so we had her pose as Allison's sister and do some poking around for us. So I guess you could say I hired you Chambers." I jerked up in my seat and shook my head "Why not just come to me straight up, why all these games?" I asked. He looked across the table at me and the expression on his face was back to business. "I don't get out much Chambers. It's not in my best interest. We played an angle. It didn't work out, so get over it!" he replied in a tone I wasn't about to challenge. Now he looked me straight in the eye "You find Allison, whatever the cost! I'm your new client Chambers and I expect results, Capisce?" I pulled on my right ear a little with my one free hand and replied "I think I've gotten a little more then I bargained for already, and besides I'm a little picky about who I take on as clients. If it's ok with you, I think I'll take a pass on this one Mr. Corrao".

He stood up out of his seat suddenly, sending the chair flying violently into the wainscot on wall behind him. He grabbed the sledge on the sideboard "che diavolo! Can you believe the balls on this shamus Joey?" he shouted at the man still sitting behind me with the gun. Joey didn't reply, but I suddenly felt the cold steel of his gun muzzle back up against my neck. "It's not ok with me!" he shouted leaning over in my face now. I could smell the wine and garlic on his breath now. "You find Allison or I let Joey plug you right here and now! What's it gonna be?"

It was an easy decision I thought to myself. It wasn't my habit to let thugs push me around, but this was different. Even if I thought I could somehow take these two with a fifty pound weight tied to my hand, I would still have to get by whatever guns he had downstairs, and they would get me eventually anyway. Maybe tomorrow, maybe next month, but they would get me someday. You can't win in the long term against these mobs. I had seen too many poor suckers gunned down on their way out of church by these gangsters. "Since you put it that way, I'll find her for you" I replied.   His body eased up a little as he sat back down "When you do, you come back to me, and no police. Joey here will keep you company" he suggested. I shook my head again. "No, I'll find her for you, but I do it my way, and by myself" I insisted. "Lugging some gunsel around with me is only going to attract attention." Corrao stood up and walked to the opposite side of the table. He picked up a piece of bread, looked over at the gunman behind me, and nodded his head. I felt the gun muzzle withdraw from the back of my neck, as his other hand appeared holding a switchblade along the side of my throat. His thumb worked the button on the side and a blade flew open from the handle. He held the blade close to my throat for a few seconds before lowering it to cut the ropes that had tied my hand to the anvil. I lifted my hand off the hunk of metal and shook the blood back into it. Joey exited the room for a moment.

A minute later he walked back into the dining room and handed me my coat and hat.   As I stood up to leave Corrao looked over at me "I'll give you twenty four hours Chambers. I'm not a patient man... You find Allison, or you'll become one of those dead ends, Capisce!" I started for the door, but hesitated for a moment in the doorway. I turned to ask one last question "Was there anything special Allison was working on, something that would have gotten her jammed up?" He looked up at me and thought about it "No, she did bullshit corporate research, wasted most of her time down at city hall or in the Providence library. I told her to quit that job and I would take care of her, but she wouldn't let it go." He took out a handkerchief from his pocket and wiped his brow for a moment as he thought it over "...she had just started some research on a story they were doing about stripers in Narragansett Bay?" he replied. "Does that help?" he asked. "It might" I replied. "But what I don't get is if you were using the girl to pull me in, why have that hunk of meat waiting out in my car last night?" He shot back a puzzled look "What the hell are you talking about Chambers?" I looked back at him "Your man Vincent, waiting out in my car last night?" I replied. He laughed a little "Hammer doesn't work for us anymore. He went freelance about a year ago. I haven't seen that crazy bastard since."

"Any idea who he might be working for now?" I questioned. "Not a clue, but that bone head is a loose cannon no matter who he's working for, that's why we let him walk" he replied. I nodded and walked out of the room.

As I walked out through the kitchen, I noticed two pots boiling over on the stovetop, and about three more bottles of the homemade red wine sitting on the kitchen table. A sawed off double barrel shotgun and a box of shells were laid out with the other utensils on the kitchen counter. I exited the kitchen through the rear door and headed down a dimly lit back stairway to the first floor. I stepped out of the back door into a modest fenced in backyard.   It was dark out now, and a dim lantern was lit just over the garage door. The rain was pouring down, and a small waterfall was gushing out of the gutter just above my head. Two tall men stood aside of the garage smoking cigarettes, each wore shoulder holsters, and each held what looked to be a snub nosed revolver inside. One said something in Italian to the other while pointing over at me. I just nodded my head at them and started walking away down the driveway. I exited the drive onto Atwells Ave into the heart of Federal Hill. I turned to notice the address on the unassuming two unit home, which read one hundred nineteen.

A yellow cab was parked about two blocks up the road. I waived it down and took it back to my apartment. I vaguely remember paying the cab driver before stumbling back upstairs to my unit a few minutes later.

The door to my apartment was still wide open. The room was dark and dead, and I could still detect the smell of cheap gangster aftershave as I walked back into my parlor and switched on the ceiling light. As the light illuminated the room, I saw that my mail was still scattered over the worn-out Oriental rug covering my parlor floor. I left it scattered. I closed the door behind me and locked it, pulling the chain securely across the latch. A minute later I staggered into the kitchen and switched on a small mission style lamp standing on top of the table. The dirty dishes from yesterday were still soaking in the sink, and the morning paper sat unread on the counter top where I had left it. I opened the cabinet just above the sink where I kept the liquor, and pulled down an old bottle of rye. I lifted a dirty cup out of the sink, poured myself half a glass, and rubbed my aching head as I drank a little down. A minute later I walked back over and opened the small cupboard just below the sink. I reached my hand underneath and pulled out an object wrapped in an old greasy towel that I kept hidden away. It was the Colt 45 that had been issued to me in the Navy. It had been a long day and I needed some rest. I wasn't about to be Shanghaied again tonight. I staggered into my bed room with the gun tucked in my waist belt and sat down on the bed. I placed the drink down on the side table and took my shoes off, fell back with my legs still hanging over the side, and let my eyes close.

Several hours later I awoke to a beam of sunlight that was poking its way through the window curtains and baking the left side of my face.   I gradually lifted my tired head and glanced over at the clock on the side table.   It was half past seven on Sunday morning. The first thought to run through my head was the twenty-four hour deadline Corrao had given me, and the realization that I had just slept through ten of them. I stood up and opened the window. A breeze of fresh morning air filled the room, and it smelt like it always did the morning after a heavy storm. A layer of fog hovered above the green grass, while moisture from the rain still hung in the air. A good ocean storm always seemed to clear the smog from the air, which seemed especially fresh this morning.

I stuck my head out the window and took a deep breath of that fresh air. Two robins chirped away at each other somewhere in the maple tree below me. I could make out the sound of some inconsiderate worker hammering on wood close by. I looked out across New London Ave. There were two young girls playing jacks in the driveway of the small cape across the street, while a boy a few years older was riding his bike up the sidewalk slinging Sunday papers across the front lawns of Journal subscribers. An older gentleman in denim jeans was walking a black Labrador up the road, and a very pretty well dressed young women in her twenties with straight brown hair sat at the bus stop just in front of my building.

Just then I noticed the car. It was parked about a block up the street on the opposite side of the road. It was the same 1939 black DeSoto I had seen in the garage two nights earlier. This time someone was seated in the front seat. I quickly jerked my head back into the window and away from his view. I waited about ten seconds and leisurely peaked around the curtain to see if I had spooked him. The car was still there, but just as I glanced back out the window I heard his engine start up.

I turned quickly and ran out of the bedroom and back through the parlor. I unlocked the front door and released the chain, which was still as I had left it the night before. I bolted into the hallway and opened the door to the stairway, lunging down several steps at a time. I reached down at my waist to see if the Colt was still there. It was still tucked under my belt, so I pulled my shirt out from my pants to hide it. I ran down from the stairway and sprinted out through the main lobby doors into the front parking lot. By the time I looked up the street he was already gone.

The pretty girl sitting at the bus stop turned and looked over her shoulder at me "Miss your bus mister?" she questioned. "There is another one coming in fifteen minutes". "No, all set… Thanks anyway" I replied, a little out of breath and began walking back towards the glass front doors of the apartment building. Just as I reached for the door handle, I noticed the women at the bus stop stand up and turn toward me through the dim reflection of the glass doors. It looked as though she was pulling an object out of her purse. She raised her hand and pointed that object at me. I instinctively dove down to the right behind two garbage cans just as a single shot ring out. The glass door shattered and collapsed into tiny pieces, most of which landed on top of me. I pulled the 45 out of my pocket and fired off two rounds over the trash barrels in her direction. Just then the DeSoto came roaring up the street and screeched to a halt in front of the bus stop. I lifted my head just in time to see the passenger side door swing open and the women diving into the front seat. The door slammed shut as the car spun its wheels and roared off down the road. I looked up at a now silent New London Ave. The birds had stopped chirping, and there was no sign of the same pedestrians I had seen just a few moments earlier. The police would be here in minutes, and I couldn't afford to spend the day downtown answering their pointless questions. I ran back up to my apartment, grabbed my jacket, hat, and keys and bolted back down into the parking lot.

Five minutes later I was driving down Post Rd heading back in the direction of Warwick. The traffic was light and I could hear the fait sound of police sirens in the distance as I drove away from the City of Cranston. I pulled over at a service station and stepped out of the car to use the pay phone. Just then a young attendant walked out of the station and called over to me "what'll it be mister?" I checked my wallet and glanced back at him "One dollar please, and could you hit the windows." He nodded his head and went to work pumping gas into my tank. I dropped a nickel in the coin slot and heard the click of a dial tone. Detective Bradley was usually off on Sundays, so I took a chance and gave the operator his home number.

The phone rang at least six times on the other end before Tom's gruffly voice came over the line "Yeah" he barked out. "Morning Tom, its Nick… I just had a little excitement down at my place, and I wanted to give you a head's up." I paused for a moment. "What type of excitement?" he questioned. "Some woman seated out at the bus stop this morning decided to take a shot at me. She jumped into a thirty-nine black DeSoto, and peeled off with another driver. It was the same black DeSoto that I had seen Friday night out at that house on Warwick Neck!" I replied. I heard a heavy sigh come over then line. "Why are you calling me with this Chambers? Didn't you tell your story to the boys when they arrived?" he asked. I paused for a moment and then continued "Look Tom... I waited around for some time, but nobody showed so I'm calling you now." I could hear a Tom swearing in the background. His voice finally came back over the phone "You listen to me good Nick. I'm telling you to get your ass down to the station pronto and file a complete report. Understand?" I took a deep breath "Listen Pal, this outfit means business! You need to grab two shields and meet me down at 1030 Warwick Neck Drive ASAP. We can't be wasting time answering senseless questions downtown." He took a moment to think it over and then responded "OK, meet me down there at 10:00am. Don't make me wait!" he commanded.

"Thanks Tom, by the way, did you ever ID that kid who washed up down on Warwick Point yesterday?" "Yeah, the kids name was Billy Gibson. Family lives down at Oakland Beach on Sea View Drive. He kept a small boat down in Brush Neck Cove. Why you asking? You think he's connected to your case?" he asked.   "I'm not sure" I replied. "To be honest I'm running a little low on leads. My client was dumped down at the shipyard, and my missing person was doing some research into a story on Narragansett Bay?" "That sounds a little thin Nick" he replied. "But check into it anyway if you like... just not today! One case at a time" he replied.

I hung up the receiver and headed back towards my car. I paid the attendant a dollar for the gas and gave him an extra dime for cleaning the windows. As I exited the service station I debated for a moment on whether I should head south towards Oakland Beach, or turn right and head north to Providence and the police.   I turned left.

Oakland Beach was a small seaside village located in Warwick along the eastern shoreline. It had a little town beach that was frequented by the locals, and there was a small cove with a dozen or so private docks where the residents kept their boats. Brush Neck Cove was also home to a handful of commercial fishing boats and lobsterman. As luck would have it was on the way to Warwick Neck.

It was about 8:30am when I drove down Oakland Beach Drive and turned right down Pinehurst Ave into Brush Neck Cove. I decided to yank the damp blanket down from my window and let some fresh air into the car. I pulled into a small dirt parking lot and parked my sedan alongside the pier. I noticed a small shack with a sign hanging on the window that read *Office*.   There wasn't much activity on the docks, and most of the boats sat quietly tied up alongside a central pier. I opened my door and stepped out of the car. A blinding sun was glimmering off the ocean and there were only scattered clouds visible now in the sky above. Three long necked geese glided by overhead without needing to flap their wings. A heavy wind was gusting off the bay, and the water out in the cove was still pretty choppy from the storm. Five foot waves were breaking down along the beach and the only person I could see was an old man with a rod cast into the surf. I helped myself to a deep breath of the fresh sea air as I shut my door and stepped up onto the pier. The smell of seaweed was stronger once I got up onto the dock.

I walked over to the office shack and knocked on the door. Almost immediately, a disheveled young man creaked open the rickety wooden door and stuck his crooked head out. "Morning" he said in a half asleep voice. He was about eighteen, wore dirty khaki shorts and a torn tee shirt. He looked scruffy, had messy hair, and I was guessing from his sleepy state that he had spent the night in the shack. "Looking for some information on Billy Gibson" I said as I pulled a card out of my pocket and handed it over to him. He gave me a confused look as he started to read the card. He finally finished reading and handed it back to me "Down on the beach, that's his dad out there fishing". He abruptly slammed the door in my face. I turned to look back at an old man standing along the water's edge. He looked to be in his early sixties, on the thin side, with gray hair and maybe six feet in height. His face was unshaven, and weathered by the sea and sun. He was wearing a dark green kaki rain jacket, and held a fishing rod in his hands. His line was cast out about 30 yards into the surf.

He was motionless as I walked down onto the beach and approached him. "Excuse me, Mr. Gibson?" I questioned as I got closer. His gaze was still cast out to the sea, but he slowly turned his attention over at me. His eyes were bloodshot red and he seemed a little unfocused at first. "Yes... do I know you?" he asked. I pulled out the same card I had shown the boy on the dock and handed it to him "No sir... I'm sorry to hear about your son. My name is Nicholas Chambers. I'm investigating a missing person's case and I believe your son's death could be connected in some way." He directed his attention back to the sea, and turned his reel in a few clicks. "There isn't much I can tell you that I haven't already gone over with those police officers." I ignored his response "I was wondering if you might have any idea why Billy would have gone out on the bay during that storm? Maybe how that type of accident could have happened? How he could have gotten tangled up in that netting?" The old man turned sharply at me "Listen here mister... that was no accident! First of all my boy was an experienced lobsterman. He'd been working out on that bay for the past ten years, and had seen much worst storms then that. He knew better then to take that twenty foot boat of his out in that type of blow. Besides, his engine was always stalling out on him. There's just no way he would have gone out alone in that weather." He paused to catch his breath for a moment. I didn't say anything. "You ever been out on a lobster boat Mr. Chambers?" he asked while squinting his left eye over at me. "I can't say that I have. I did some time in the Navy but that was a long ways from a lobster boat." I replied.

He bent forward and jammed the fishing pole into the sand "Follow me young man!" he said with some authority. He walked in front of me heading back across the beach, and made his way slowly up the steps onto the dock I had just descended from. He stepped onto a smaller dock that had about a dozen or so medium sized boats tied to it. He strolled out to the end of the dock and stepped onto one of the larger boats, which was tied off second from the end. It was and old wooden boat painted white with blue trim, maybe thirty-five feet in length. The name *Misty Blue* was painted on the stern of the boat. "Watch your step young man" he said, while reaching his hand out to me and helping me to climb aboard.

The boat had a central pilot house with a steering wheel and large windows around all sides. Towards the bow of the boat there was an undersized sleeping cuddy with two tiny windows on either side. A dozen wooden lobster pots were stacked in the stern. The old man turned and sat up against the side rail "This is my boat Mr. Chambers. She's thirty-six feet in length. Billy's boat was just over twenty-one feet bow to stern. Let me ask you something, do you see any fishing nets?" I took a quick glance around "None... just rope and traps" I replied. He grinned a little and looked back at me "You know why that is Mr. Chambers?" I nodded and replied "Because you're a lobsterman, not a fisherman." The somber look that had occupied his face suddenly gave way to a smile. I tugged on my right earlobe and tilted my head "Did you tell all this to the police?" He gazed back at me "Sure did... they said it was still probably just a fishing accident."

He stood up and walked into the cabin. I heard some keys jingle, and suddenly I heard the boat's engine roar to life as water began gurgling back towards the stern. He called back out to me "Did they teach you how to cast off lines in the Navy?" I took my jacket off and replied "They did." I untied the lines and stowed them away, and within few seconds two twin screws came to life in the rear of the boat and began propelling us out to sea.

We headed out through Brush Neck Cove, passed
by Oakland Beach Point and made our way onto
Greenwich Bay.   The water was getting pretty
choppy the further out we went. I sat on top of
several weathered lobster pots in the stern, but was
getting bounced up out of my seat every few
seconds. I had a clear view of the old man steering
the boat in the pilot house. His back was turned
away from me, looking out towards the bow of the
boat. He navigated out through the channel
markers as he had probably done thousands of
times before.   "Bout five to ten foot swells right
now... was nearly double that night before last." he
shouted back to me. I still wasn't sure where he was
taking me, but I got his point. There was no way
Billy would have taken a boat half the size of this
one out onto the Bay with swells twice the size of
the ones that were knocking me over right now.
He took us out around the tip of Warwick point and
cut the engines just before reaching the north end of
Prudence Island.

I could see a dozen or so colored lobster pot
markers bobbing up and down out of the clear blue
water. The old man grabbed a long handled boat
hook off the wall in the pilot house. He walked
back out to me and leaned over the starboard side of
the boat. Within a few seconds he had hooked one
of the markers and was pulling the wet rope back

up onto the deck. After about thirty feet of rope, a
wooden lobster pot emerged out from the water
"Give me a hand young man" he said as he grabbed
a hold of the pot. I leaned over the side and
grabbed onto one end of the wooden frame. Just as
I did a large swell came and knocked me off me feet
back into the boat. I coughed up some sea water as
I sat up on the damp floor. The old man was still
standing at the side of the boat and pulled the trap
up over the boat's edge, then dropped it back down
onto the floor. "Thought you said you were a Navy
man?" He laughed at me. I stood up slowly and
replied "Didn't see much time top side" and laughed
back a little. I took a good look down at the trap,
which had several occupants inside. He opened the
top of the pot and reached his weathered bare hand
in to remove the lobsters. He dropped them into a
large bucket that was filled with salt water, closed
the pot back up, and hoisted the empty trap over
the side throwing it back into the sea. The rope on
the floor quickly uncoiled itself back into the water
as the trap sank to the ocean floor.

He sat down on one of the weathered teak benches
along the side of the boat. I stood up and held onto
the cabin door for balance as the boat bobbed up
and down in rhythm with the swells. "Who would
want to kill your son Mr. Gibson?" I abruptly
asked. He rubbed the back of his neck for a
moment "Some trouble started about a month ago.

This big tanker out of Argentina had steered out from the channel markers one night and dropped anchor right about here." He rubbed his neck a little more. "We drop most of our traps in this area, so Billy took a run out in his boat that night to try to get them to shove off. When he got out here he said they had a couple of frog men diving in the water to fix a broken prop. The ship pulled anchor about two hours later and steered back into the channel heading for Providence, dragging half a dozen of our traps with her." He leaned over the side and spit into the ocean. "Seemed innocent enough at first… But just last week the same ship pulled off here again at Warwick Point dredging up more of our pots." My head shot up. I hadn't realized where we were drifting to. Dead ahead just off the bow was Warwick Lighthouse, which sat directly at the tip of Warwick Point and Warwick Neck Drive. The old man kept talking "Billy shot out there again that night, this time with a huge flood light. I could hear him shouting at the crew on deck and shining the light all over the ship. They were screaming back at him, but he couldn't make out much of what they were saying since they were all speaking in some foreign language. There was one man who spoke English, just swearing at Billy and telling him to clear out."

I leaned against the pilot cabin, pulled a cigarette out of my pocket and lit it up "You told all this to the police?" I questioned. He looked back over at

me "Sure as hell did!" "What did they say?" I asked.
He shrugged his shoulders and shook his head a
little "They think it was a fishing accident." I took
another drag of my cigarette "You didn't happen to
get the name of the ship?" I asked. "She was named
the Argentine Mist" he replied. The name was
familiar to me. I probed a little deeper "Did you
contact the Coast Guard to report any of this?" He
stood up and started back for the pilot cabin "No,
that's what I told him to do, but that dam reporter
said she would take care of it for him. Good for
nothing reporters. Only interested in their dam
stories!" He passed by me and walked back into the
pilot house. Just then I heard the engines come to
life. I tossed my but overboard and followed him
into the pilot cabin. "Was the reporter named
Allison Baxter?" I questioned with my case hanging
on the line. The air inside the pilot house was stale
and not as fresh as the ocean air just inches outside.
He looked back over his shoulder at me "Yeah that
was her name alright. How did you know?" he
questioned. "Your reporter is my missing person" I
replied. His brushy grey eyebrows rose a little just
before his hand threw the boat into gear and we
began powering forward again.

I looked out through the smudgy windows of his
pilot house up at the coast line along Warwick Neck
"Are you familiar with this coast captain?" I asked.
He looked back at me and nodded, wondering

where my question was headed. "Could you get me close to 1030 Warwick Neck? It's a small bungalow up on the cliff with a widow's walk on top. Has an old wooden stairway and rail leading down to a dock along the rocks. Know it?" I questioned. He didn't respond, just swung the wheel around and throttled the engine into high gear. We made our way around to the east side of Warwick neck, which looked out across Narragansett Bay towards Riverside. "You really think this has something to do with my boy's death?" he asked. "Too much coincidence not to be linked in some way" I replied.

Within three minutes we were pulling up to the same makeshift dock I had seen two nights before from the cliff above. The dock was more visible now. It was fixed to some large rocks and built out from the shoreline along the base of the cliff. The swells were heavy, but not large enough to submerge the dock as they had done during the storm. "Better take those fancy shoes off" he said. "You're better off barefoot on those rocks." I did as he said, took my shoes and socks off, and rolled up my pants. I walked back out into the fresh air towards the stern of the boat. The old man navigated up to the side and held the boat about three feet from the platform. I held my shoes under one arm and climbed back onto the stern of the boat "I'll be in touch Mr. Gibson, thanks for the lift" I shouted back as I jumped across onto the dock. I took a few steps over the platform and started up the rocks towards the stairway. By the time I had turned my head back the Misty Blue had already turned about and was motoring away from the shoreline.

12:   Bay View

As I approached the wooden stairway I noticed a black rope that was strung up along the railing through a series of eye screws in the rail posts.   I sat down on the first stair and put my shoes and socks back on.   I stood up and took a good look at the cliff.   The stairway was steep with maybe a hundred or so steps that climbed about seventy-five feet up the side of the cliff.   The rope weaved its way along the rail, up the embankment, over the top and out of sight.   I started to make my way up the stairway, which looked as though it had been severely weathered by the sea over the years.   It was badly rotted out in certain places.   The steps were steep and clung to the side of the cliff.   When I got about half way up I looked back and noticed just how high and steep the cliff was.   I decided not to look down and kept moving up.

I reached the top a couple of minutes later, and laid flat on my stomach over the last few stairs.   The wind seemed to be gusting heavily now at the edge of the cliff, and I took one last look down the side of the embankment.   I reached into my shoulder holster and unlatched the snap securing my forty-five.   This outfit had got the jump on me twice already, and I wasn't taking any more chances. There was a small gate at the top, the kind you usually see with these beach house stairways.   I spotted a small bell tied to the end of the black rope hanging inside the gate. I peered up over the top step to get a better look at the small bungalow I had visited two nights earlier. It was as I had left it, although it looked slightly bigger in the daylight. From my vantage point I could see a side family room with a fireplace that I hadn't noticed before. I looked over towards the driveway to see if Detective Bradley had arrived with backup yet, but the drive was empty. I watched the house for about three minutes trying to spot any sign of life inside, but nothing moved.

After a few minutes, I stood up on the stairs and casually opened the gate. I walked across the back lawn and stepped up on the back porch. The porch floor was worn and weathered. The hand railing was falling off its hinges and some old faded newspapers were lying aside of a navy blue Adirondack chair up on the porch. I approached the back screen door, opened it, and peered through the door's window into a small kitchen. I could see and old gas stove and a small kitchen table with two chairs. The counter and sink were just to the right of the door and a small fringe was tucked in the left corner of the room. There were no signs of life coming from inside. I gave the door a good knock and waited. Still nothing. I banged a little loader now with the side of my fist and shouted to anyone inside "Hey, anybody home inside!" Nobody responded. I gave it another minute and then tried at the door knob, which was locked. I took a look at my watch. It was 9:15am, so I knew I had a good thirty minutes before Tom arrived. The kitchen had a window looking out at the back porch. I stepped over to it and tried to push it up, but it was latched on the inside. I pulled the gun out of my shoulder holster and tapped its metal handle through one of the top window panes. The glass broke easily, and I passed my hand inside to unfasten the latch. I lifted the window open and climbed inside.

It was dark in the kitchen and the smell of cigarettes permeated the room. Several ash trays sat on the table full of half smoked buts. The sink was full of unwashed soiled dishes, while an uncovered iron pot sat on the stove with overcooked beans that had been overcooked for some time. I listened for a moment, but there was only silence. "Hello, anyone home? Police!" I shouted out. Still nothing. I eased my gun back in its holster, and walked over to the ice box. I opened the door and saw three empty shelves with a few cans of beer. I helped myself to one and closed the door. A minute later I walked into a musty living room that had a baby grand Steinway sitting next to a large bay window. Sheet music which had not been played in years sat on cherry bench tucked underneath the piano. High curtains made of Chinese silk with a landscape pattern hung from the window on the opposite wall. A small Victorian clock ticked away on the mantelpiece, while the rest of the room listened intently. I walked through the living room and stepped down into the jut out family room I had noticed from the yard.

The room dropped one step down from the parlor, and all of the shades were drawn tightly closed. I walked across the spacious floor and let the shades snap up violently. Daylight invaded the previously murky room. It was completely empty aside from a small fold up wooden chair and a telescope on a tripod positioned aside of it.   There was a large fireplace on the opposite side of the room that was surrounded by flagstones covering nearly half the wall. The telescope was pointed out one of the windows looking down towards Narragansett Bay. I stooped over and peered into the lens of the narrow instrument, pointing it down in the direction of the water.   It was unfocused, and I decided to leave it that way. I turned the telescope and started scanning across the bay. A large barge was making its way up the channel directly in front of the house. I pointed the scope towards the slowly moving ship, but the image was still blurry. I swung the scope southward and scanned around the bay to see if I could find a focal point. It took a few minutes but after a moment or so one area came clearly into focus. The land was familiar to me. The Quonset Point Naval Station had just been commissioned in July of this year, and was quickly becoming a major base for the US military. The scope was perfectly focused on the base and two large destroyers tied up alongside the pier. My case just became much more interesting.

I walked back up into the open parlor and headed up a small narrow stairway into a loft bedroom. There were two small unmade twin sized beds on either side of the room. There was a mildewed stench lingering in the room, while the ceilings arched down on either side as they usually do in most bungalows. A single large twelve pane window hung at the back of the room overlooking the bay. A pink porcelain lamp with a horse and beagle sat waiting for the hunt to begin on the window sill. The lamp had a dark green glass globe covering its light bulb. On the opposite side of the room a spiral staircase led up to the widows walk that was visible from the outside. I turned the lamp on. The bulb was extremely bright and lit up the room with a bright green light that blinded me momentarily. I flipped the switch off and let my eyes adjust back to the dimly lit room. I walked over to the spiral staircase and started climbing. There was a small hatch at the top going through the ceiling, which was locked on the inside. I unlatched the lock and pushed the hatch up, flipping it over and onto the roof. Rays of brilliant sunlight suddenly filled the previously gloomy room. Just above the hatch was a small pull down ladder that was secured to the roof. I pulled down the telescopic metal ladder and started to climb up.

The sun was extremely bright outside, and my eyes needed to adjust again as I stepped out onto the sun baked roof. The widow's walk was about fifteen feet in length and extended about five feet wide. There was an old wooden railing just three feet in height built around the walkway to prevent sightseers from tumbling down onto the roof. I stood up fully and took a good look around the property. The back of the house faced eastward out onto Narragansett Bay. It was an unbelievable view of the ocean, and allowed you to see all the way to East Providence and as far south as Jamestown. The smell of salt water permeated the air, and the wind seemed to be gusting at much higher speeds above the house. The front yard faced the West and looked out into the woods towards Warwick Neck Drive. The small dingy garage I had visited two nights earlier was about fifty yards to the left of the house, and the entire property was in need of some overdue landscaping work. The house itself was completely isolated and out of sight from the main road. It was a perfect place for someone not wanting to be found to do just that.

Just then I saw two vehicles making their way up the long dirt driveway towards the house. Lingering dust clouds puffed up from behind the cars as they approached. I crouched down and pulled the automatic out from my shoulder holster to see who it was. In a few seconds I could see it was Detective Bradley with an unmarked squad car following in the rear. Both cars approached slowly and drove up the driveway near the back porch I had made my entrance through.

The cars stopped and turned their engines off. Several large men stepped out of the two vehicles and made their way up onto the back porch. I heard some pounding on the back door, and someone shout out "Police, open up!" A minute or so passed while I heard some quiet talking taking place on the porch.   Just then I heard what sounded like someone kicking in the back door, the sound of wood splintering, followed by a load crash.   I walked back over to the roof hatch and listened to what was happening down below. Footsteps shuffled around on the first floor, and within a minute or two someone was walking up the steps into the bedroom below me. "Up here Tom" I shouted out. The iron ladder began rattling and soon Detective Bradley's head emerged up through the hatch. He didn't look happy. "Tell me someone let you in here Chambers?" he said a little short of breath as he stepped up onto the roof. "Door was wide open, but nobody home at the moment" I replied. He shook his head in disgust "Give me a reason not to arrest you right now for B&E. You can't just go barging into people's homes half cocked on your own. Half the force is out there searching the city for you, and your apartment manager just filled out a complaint against you downtown. He said it's not the first time there's been gun play since you moved in. You better give me what you've got right now, or I need to take you in Nick!"

I pulled out a cigarette and handed it to him, then took one out for myself. I lit mine first and tossed him the lighter as I leaned up against the old railing on the widows walk. "My client hired me on Friday to find her missing sister. She ended up dead yesterday along with that young boy from Oakland Beach. Oh, and by the way, he wasn't a fisherman, he was a lobsterman. Spoke with his dad earlier, turns out he had a beef with a tanker out off Warwick Point about a month ago. They were parking on his livelihood and he let them know what he thought about it. Either way, it wasn't any fishing accident, that's for sure... He was just too experienced to go out in that blow. Anyway, I woke up this morning to see that same Black DeSoto from Friday night parked out in front of my apartment. I ran out to see what gives, but the car had already taken off. As I'm walking back inside some young thing sitting at the bus stop takes a shot at me and then jumps into the DeSoto and peels off. So I thought it would make some sense to come back down here and pay these jokers a visit." I looked over at Detective Bradley who was smoking his cigarette and looking out down towards the water. I hadn't given him everything because I didn't want the police banging around my case before I had a chance to solve it. But it was hopefully enough for him to cut me some slack for a while. "OK Nick, but you're going to have to come down and speak with the Captain, tell him what you just told me" he replied. I tossed my half smoked cigarette off the roof and replied "I've only got half a story now Tom, give me a little time and I'll get the rest for you. That way it will play better with your Captain." He kept staring out down towards the water and hesitated for about a minute... "OK, but be sure to get your ass down to the station first thing in the morning, and don't make me regret this Nick."

We both turned and began to climb down the latter back into the musty bedroom below. We walked across the room without speaking and headed down the narrow stairway back into the parlor on the first floor. Just then, a young officer with short dirty-brown hair emerged from a doorway, which presumably led down to the basement. "Pretty empty down their Detective, just found these on a workbench. There's really nothing else to see." The young officer handed Dave a small stack of white three by four papers, which looked like the kind used for printing photographs. "Ok, how about the garage?" he questioned. The young officer starred over at me for a moment, probably wondering where I had materialized from. "Empty, nothing out there but some old oil cans and a tool bench." he replied. Tom looked over at me "Well what do you think Nick? Looks like whoever they were they've cleared out." "Yeah, seems that way" I replied without much expression. He turned back at me "What kind of racket you figure this for Nick?" I scratched the back of my neck a little "can't say for certain yet, but these monkeys aren't here on vacation, that's for sure." I replied. "Well, we'll try to find out who owns the house." he said. Just then a second older officer with salt and pepper hair entered the room "Call for you on the radio sir." Tom turned towards him and replied "I'll be right out Jim." He turned his attention back to me "Tomorrow morning Nick, don't be late, and have your facts straight!" I nodded and he exited the room with the second officer. The two men walked outside and got back into one of the cars. I heard some talking over the police radio, and then an engine starting up. A few seconds later the car was driving away. I turned to the younger officer "How about a lift Jack?" He nodded and ten minutes later we were headed down Warwick Neck drive back towards Oakland Beach.

The officer dropped me off with my car down at
Brush Neck Cove.   I noticed the Misty Blue was tied
back up in its slip already. I looked back down
towards the beach, but Mr. Gibson's tackle box and
fishing pole were no longer there. I jumped in my
car, pulled at the choke, and started the engine. I
still had one major lead I needed to follow up on.
The address on the DeSoto's registration had been
for an Arnold Strauss at 210 Blackstone Boulevard
up on the East Side of Providence. That was one of
the facts I neglected to tell Detective Bradley. I still
wasn't sure exactly how these people were
connected to my missing person's case, and I knew
Corrao was expecting some answers by the end of
the day. But I couldn't have this mob taking pot
shots at me while I followed up on Allison. She had
called me yesterday morning… so she was most
likely just lying low somewhere. In the meantime,
this crew was getting on my nerves. I headed for
the East Side.

By the time I reached Blackstone Boulevard it was
just about noontime.   Blackstone Boulevard ran
along the Upper East Side of Providence, and was
home to many wealthy and elite citizens of the city.
Large private walls surrounded lavish oversized
estates along the boulevard, while tall oak trees
adorned the road on either side. The homes on the
eastern side of the street faced down onto the

Blackstone River, which flowed from Pawtucket down through Providence and out into Narragansett Bay. I reached 210 Blackstone Boulevard, which was a large Tudor estate situated far behind a six foot red brick wall that lined the perimeter of the property. A winding driveway curved its way across a perfectly manicured green lawn back up to the main house. There was a large black wrought iron front gate that secured the entrance to the estate located at the end of the driveway. A small gate house sat just behind the stone wall inside the front gate. The initials *AS* were welded onto the front of each gate painted in white, while gold leaf arrow tips protruded up from each of the posts along the gate. A gray weathered iron eagle with wings spread topped the middle of the gate, while a large metal latch secured its center.

I decided to park my Olds out on the boulevard in front of the property and walk up to the front entrance. There was a small doorbell just to the right of the gate above a mailbox drop. I pushed it and immediately heard a buzzer sound from inside the gatehouse. Just then I heard dogs barking and within a few seconds two German Sheppard's came sprinting out from the main house. They raced up to the gate and began showing off their teeth to me. A minute or so passed before an old man came walking out from behind the gatehouse. "Down boys... Down now!" he shouted out as he approached the other side of the gate. "Good afternoon, can I help you?" he questioned. He was a short skinny oriental man who looked to be in his early seventies. He wore denim overalls and a dirty navy blue tee shirt. His hands were rough, covered with soil, and looked like they had been working most of their lives. He wore bug eyed spectacles that enlarged his eyes, and his face was unshaven and sweaty. He squinted at me through the iron gate.

I pulled out a tin badge I had bought down at the five and dime "Police, here to see Mr. Strauss" I said in a commanding way. "You have appointment?" he questioned. "No appointment necessary when it's police business" I replied. He shot me a nasty look "Name?" "Detective Chambers… Now open this gate up" I ordered. He grabbed both dogs by their collar and walked them back into the gatehouse. Two minutes later he emerged from the small house and walked back over to unlatch the gate. He worked the lever and pulled the iron bolt across and out of its retaining slot. He stepped back and pulled the creaking gate back into the driveway. I stepped through the entrance and onto the cement drive.

There was a small sidewalk along one side, so I started my way up the winding driveway towards the main house. As I walked up, I noticed a triple garage built off the right side of the house. There was a white convertible Cadillac parked in front, and the last garage door was wide open at the moment. I turned back to see if the gardener was still watching, but he had retired back into his gatehouse. I strolled quickly up the front path and climbed the steps to an oversized oak front door, which had an interesting eight panel stained glass window in its top section. There was a tarnished brass knocker in the shape of a lion's head bolted to the center of the door. The lion was holding the knocker handle in his teeth. I grabbed at the brass handle and gave a few solid knocks up against the door. A long minute passed without a response so I gave the door a few more knocks.

A shadowy image began to appear through the stained glass. The shadow moved closer to the door until I could hear a lock clicking on the inside. The large door swung open and a striking woman in her early thirties stood in the doorway. She was about 5"10' in height with a slim figure and innocent looking face. Her platinum blonde hair was pulled back into a long pony tail that reached well over her shoulders, and her eyes were teal green. She wore a dark brown blouse with a white lace collar, and a tight black silk skirt that showed off her hips. Sheer stockings covered her slim legs, and a pair of pink reading glasses hung down from her slender neck. She looked me up and down before speaking. "Yes?" was all she said. I flipped my toy badge out of its wallet, being careful to keep a few fingers over it while showing it to her through the screen "Police Miss, here to see Mr. Strauss." An uneasy look came over her innocent face. She glanced back over her shoulder for a moment but quickly returned her attention to me. "Please, won't you come inside officer?" she said as she unlocked the screen door and opened it for me.

I stepped into the oversized front hallway, which had an impressive twenty-five foot plaster ceiling. An enormous crystal chandelier hung from the center of the ceiling above. The hallway extended back towards the rear of the house, with half a dozen six panel doors situated along it. A large mahogany stairway with hunter green carpeting tacked up its center rolled down into the front hallway. Some twenty or so wide-cut steps climbed up to a middle level platform, while two separate stairways on either side hugged the walls connecting the platform to the second floor. The floor in the main hallway was made of black Italian marble with grains of white bleeding through. A large maple Biedermeier grandfather clock stood watch to the left of the stairway. An angel's face with wings was carved just below the clock's rooftop. On the wall to the left hung a large expressionist painting of a woman with long black hair. She was dressed in a sheer black silk number lying comfortably on a couch. Her head rested on a colorful pillow, while a long bead of white pearls adorned her neck and draped down below her waist.   Her small ruby lips were shut tight leaving her face expressionless.

The women opened a door just off of the hallway "Please wait in the library while I try to find my uncle. What did you say your name was officer?" she asked as she began to make her way up the ornate stairway.   "Detective Chambers, Ma'am" I replied as I let myself into the room. The library was spacious with ceiling to floor bookshelves lining the walls on two sides of the enormous room. A three section large bay window protruded out from the back wall, letting sunlight flood through most of the room.   The ceiling was adorned with a dark cherry dental crown molding, and heavy velvet drapes with gold crosses stitched inside hung on either side of the bay window. Two brown leather easy chairs sat in front of a large rustic stone fireplace on the opposite wall.

A small coffee table was positioned between the two chairs, along with a nineteenth century oak writing desk that was leaning up against the wall to the left of the fireplace. I walked over to the desk and tried to flip the cover down. It had a small lock at the top, but I noticed a small skeleton key in a candy bowl sitting on top of the desk next to a Bell telephone. I tried the key in the lock and it opened, so I pulled the thin desk cover down.   I noticed some writing paper under an ink blotter, along with a small bottle of black ink. Dozens of letters and correspondence were stacked to the left inside of the desk.   The top envelope was addressed to Mr. Arnold Strauss, 210 Blackstone Blvd, Providence, RI and was postmarked from a Robert Kregg of Hot Springs, South Dakota. The envelope below it was postmarked from someone living in Tampa, Florida. Just above the correspondence was a small shelf which held several unsharpened pencils and more writing paper.

There were two narrow drawers located on either side of the desk. I pulled at the miniature brass handle of drawer to the right, but it was locked tight. I couldn't see a key anywhere to open it. The second drawer on the left side was unlocked so I pulled it open.   A single item inside the drawer immediately caught my attention. It was a narrow metal clip belonging to an automatic pistol. I pulled it out to get a better look at it, and eight bullets were still loaded inside. The bullets looked to be 9mm, but I didn't recognize the narrow angled clip.   Just then I heard footsteps coming down the stairs out in the hallway. I set the clip back inside the drawer and closed the cover to the writing desk. I locked it up and placed the tiny key back in the candy bowl. I walked over to the bay window and admired the backyard view.

At that moment the door swung open and a tall lofty man in his early sixties strolled slowly into the room. He was partially balding with jet black hair on top and gray hair slicked back on either side of his head. He had a narrow face with a protruding chin and distinctive beaked nose. He wore a pair of tan slacks and a white button up collared shirt. An unlit cigarette was hanging from his shriveled lips, and he carried a small cocker spaniel in his left arm, which he placed on the floor as he entered the room.

"Good afternoon detective. My name is Arnold Strauss... How may I help you?" he said as he extended his hand out to me. "Hello Mr. Strauss" I replied as I shook his hand. "Just have a few questions we need to ask." He gestured to me to sit in one of the easy chairs. "Can I get you something to drink Detective?" he offered as he sat down in the chair opposite me. "No thank you" I replied. "This should only take a few minutes." He reached out to offer me a cigarette from a stainless steel case that had the initials *A.S.* engraved on it. I slid one out of the case and lifted up a large crystal lighter on the side table that must have weighed a solid pound. I lit the cigarette and continued on "Do you own a black 1939 DeSoto?" I asked. He paused for a moment before answering. "We did own one, sold it about three months ago, why do you ask Detective?" I ignored his question as cops usually do "We're going to need to know who you sold it to." He stood up and paced the room for a moment racking his brain for a name. "We sold it to a young man who had been working here for us. We had to let him go a few months ago. My wife felt bad for him and let him purchase the old DeSoto from us. His name was James."

I took another drag from my cigarette "Did James have a last name?" I asked somewhat sarcastically. He looked back over at me "ah... Smith, if I'm not mistaken. Yes, James Smith." I looked back at him "Of course it was..." I replied. "Can I ask why you let him go?" He rubbed the back of his neck sat back down in the easy chair and stalled for a moment. He looked over at the unlit fireplace and took another drag on his cigarette. "I can't recall offhand. Maybe if you told me what this was about I could be a little more helpful to you?" he replied.

"We're investigating two murders. Do you own any property out on Warwick Neck Ave?" I asked. He seemed unshaken "No, I can't say that we do" he replied while lifting the cocker spaniel up off the floor and placing it on his lap. I pressed on "Have you ever heard of a ship named the Argentine Mist? She's tied up down at the Providence Pier right now." He shook his head again looking down at the floor "No... Should I have?" he questioned. "I couldn't say, that's the point to asking questions" I replied. "Do you own a gun Mr. Strauss?" He stood up suddenly "I'm not sure I like your tone or your questions Detective. What Division did you say you worked in? I play golf with Mayor Roberts each Saturday morning, and I want to be sure I have your name right." I stood up from my seat "I don't

believe I did say. Your daughter has my name.
You'll be hearing from us. Don't bother to get up,
I'll see myself out." I replied as I walked abruptly
out of the room.

I stepped out across the large marble hallway, and
exited through the front door.   As I came down the
outside stairway I noticed the door to the last
garage was still open, and headed in its direction.
As I started to approach the first door a voice from
behind me called out "The exit is back that way
Detective." I turned to see Strauss standing on the
front steps and pointing back to the main gate.   "My
mistake" I replied as I turned and starting walking
back in the direction of the gatehouse. I looked back
up over my shoulder at one point and he was still
standing tall on the steps watching me.   As I
approached the main gate I noticed the gardener
standing next to it, ready and waiting with one of
the gates already open for me. As I passed by him I
tipped my hat and he just nodded.   I was only few
steps onto the street when I heard the gate slam
shut and the sound of it being latched from inside.

I started back up the road towards my car. I
glanced over at the high wall protecting the
property, which rose about six feet in height. I was
six feet two, so I strolled up beside it to take a look
over the ledge. In about twenty yards the wall took
a sharp ninety degree turn down onto the side

street, and then worked its way back about 200 yards to the end of the property near the Blackstone River. Tall oak trees lined the wall on the outside along the side street. A large weeping willow sat gently in the center of the well groomed back yard. Fifty yards back a stone wall dropped the yard down several feet before it slopped down into the Blackstone River. The half wall ran along the entire length of the back yard. I walked a little further down Blackstone Boulevard passing by my parked car, and turned right onto the shaded side street. I strolled casually down the road for about fifty yards and lifted my head over the old brick wall.

The half wall was right in front of me, stepping the yard down about three feet. I took a good look around the yard and up towards the house, but no one was in sight. A sturdy branch from one of the oak trees was protruding out over the wall. I grabbed a hold of the branch and swung myself up and over. I crouched down low next to the tree's base for a few minutes just to be sure no one had seen me. After a moment, I started off along the base of the wall, keeping low as I made my way across the back yard. About mid-way across the yard there was a stone stairway with five or six steps leading up to the main level. I crawled up onto the stairs and peered over the top. I could see the bay window jutting out from the library, and Strauss was standing next to the writing desk speaking on the telephone. He seemed to be shouting at someone on the other end and pounding his hand on the desk. I had rattled him alright. The back of the garage was about ten yards to my left on the opposite side of the main house. I could make a dash for it and stay out of his line of sight, but I wasn't sure where the girl was. Strauss had also mentioned a wife. So I decided to play it safe and continued crawling along the base of the wall keeping low and out of sight.

I reached the edge of the property on the opposite side, and pulled myself up over the short wall into the upper back yard. I hugged the exterior brick wall and made my way from tree to tree until I got close to the garage. I was completely out of view to anyone inside the house now, but anyone over by the gate house would still be able to see me. I saw the old man on his knees in the garden with his back facing me. Even if he turned to look, I'm not sure he would be able to see anything with those coke bottle glasses. I stood up and strolled calmly across the yard towards the garage.

There was a window on the side of the garage behind some shrubs. I walked behind the hedges and ducked down low beside the window and peered inside. The white convertible was parked in the garage now, directly in front of me in the third spot. The garage door was still open. A black Oldsmobile sat in the garage next to the convertible.

Its hood was lifted up and it looked as though someone had been working on the engine. A small red toolbox was lying on the garage floor next to the right front tire. On the opposite side of the garage a black DeSoto sat innocently in the first spot. It was dark on that end of the garage but I could easily determine the make and model of the vehicle. It was definitely the same DeSoto that had made the drive by my apartment this morning, and had been parked out in that garage on Warwick Neck Friday night. Just then two voices in the driveway approached the third open garage. I crouched a little lower, but kept peeping through the window pane.

It was Strauss, he was talking to another man that I recognized right away. It was the same man I had left handcuffed to a loading dock during the storm two nights earlier. I could hear Strauss saying something now "Remove all identification and dump the car into the river tonight" he ordered. "Make sure you remove the plates and scrape the serial number." Vincent nodded obediently and then replied "I want extra for this... and for the other thing. I got it coming to me and today's payday Strauss!" Strauss shot a disgusted look back towards the Hammer "You'll be well paid... in time" he replied. The Hammer suddenly grabbed him by the throat, lifting him slightly off the ground with one hand "I'll be well paid today!" he threatened. Strauss's face began to turn a slight shade of purple as he nodded his head in approval. Vincent let go of his throat and Strauss fell back a little gagging and catching his breath back. "Very well, come back in the house with me and I'll get your money. But this will conclude our engagement Mr. Palaeno!" He staggered out of the garage rubbing at his throat and the Hammer followed close behind.

I waited a moment and stood up from my crouched position. I walked up to edge of the garage and poked my head around the corner just in time to see the front door closing. I quickly snuck around into the garage through the open door. The top was still down on the Cadillac, so I pulled open the door and sat down in the passenger seat. I flipped down the glove compartment and several papers dropped out. It was mostly paperwork on the car's registration and insurance information. The car was registered to Beatrice Strauss of Blackstone Boulevard in Providence, who I assumed was his wife. I fanned through the paperwork, but it all seemed routine enough. I placed the papers back where I had found them and stepped back out of the Cadillac. I walked over to check out the Oldsmobile, but all of the doors were locked and the windows were shut tight. I took a look through one of the windows, and noticed a small envelope tucked under the visor on the driver's side. It was addressed to Strauss with a foreign postmark. I couldn't make out exactly where it was from, but I decided it I needed to get a closer look at it.

I peered around and noticed a hammer hanging on a hook by the workbench in the back of the garage. I grabbed the hammer and walked over to the driver's side of the Olds. I tapped the vent window lightly with the ball end, and the glass broke into the car. Just then I heard the front door open again, and footsteps began making their way down the front steps. I reached in quickly, grabbed the letter from under the visor and tucked it away in my jacket pocket. The garage door wasn't an option for exit now. There was a small back door to the garage, but I only had seconds. I drew my gun out and crouched down low behind the Olds. Within a few seconds the footsteps made their way into the garage. I stayed low and silent, and looked underneath the car at the large size twelve feet standing aside of the Cadillac. A lit cigarette dropped to the ground and one of the large shoes squashed it out. As he started to move back towards the rear of the car, I inched up to the front of the Olds. He soon stepped back out onto the driveway, and within seconds the garage door was rolling down. When it hit the ground, the latch in the Center turned and locked the door. The garage quickly became dark, aside from some light passing through the shrubs in side window.

I stood still for a moment. Finally I heard the sound of a lighter flipping open and flint being struck, followed by heavy footsteps stomping their way up the driveway. I stood up and walked over to the back door, unlocked it, and inched it open. I stepped out into the back yard, closed the door behind me, and walked along the back side of the garage. I peered around the corner and ran across to the yard to the side wall. I quickly lifted myself up and over, and landed back down on the opposite side street. It took me a good ten minutes to walk around the parameter of the property to where I had parked my car. I hopped in and sped off.

I headed back down Blackstone Boulevard in the direction of Providence. I needed to take a closer look at the letter, and I was guessing the Corrao's boys were camped out at my apartment or office. So I decided to pay a visit to the Providence Library. It was 1:30pm on Sunday afternoon, and they usually stayed open until 6:00pm on the weekends. I pulled up at the library and parked my car in the back.   The Providence Library was a 50,000 square foot two story renaissance style granite building located on Washington Street in Providence. The library was built in 1900 and housed over 90,000 books. It was a free resource that I frequently used in my line of work. I walked in through a set of double doors located in the back of the building. There was a large red headed women in her fifties seated at a central information desk in the main lobby. She looked up at me momentarily and then went back to her reading. Two young boys were splashing water over by the water fountain, while an elderly man sat quietly reading a book on a small chair in a darkened corner.

I made my way up a white marble staircase with an elaborate black wrought iron railing.   It led to the second floor reference area. The second floor walls were draped with bookshelves that rose from floor to ceiling, and the interior hallway looked down onto an open first floor. Twenty foot high arched windows stood proudly around the perimeter of the second floor, illuminating the building with natural light from the outside. I found a vacant desk in a private corner and took a seat.

I took the letter out from my jacket pocket. The tattered envelop was postmarked from Mar del Plata, Buenos Aires, Argentina, and was dated only a week ago. The envelope had already been opened but a hand written letter was still folded away inside. I pulled the paper out to take a closer look at it. It was a short one paragraph letter dated October 2nd from a Sofia Lopez. The letter read;

Dear Cousin

Enjoyed your visit last month. Looking forward to visiting you in America over the holidays, and will plan to stay for about ten days. I wanted to let you know I passed my examination to enter the Buenos Aires Academy of Music last week. They made me play Mozart's Piano Concerto number twenty-one, but I did Ok with it. I also have three new books I know you will be interested in reading, and will be sure to bring them when I come. Can't wait to see you again, maybe we can visit the Statue of Liberty in New York if we have time.

Love always,

Sofia

Sofia Lopez

1862 Av Fortunato de la Plaza

Mar del Plata, Buenos Aires, Argentina

41.666-71.378

I reread the letter several times. Parts of the puzzle were starting to come together. A letter from a cousin in Argentina; Billy Gibson's run in with the Argentine Mist out near Warwick Point; Strauss's car parked in the garage out on Warwick Neck; and Charlottes body found behind the warehouse directly across from the pier where the Mist was docked. Whatever racket these boys were running Strauss was clearly involved, but I still needed to tie things together.

I decided to have someone else take a look at the letter. I stashed the note in my pocket, got up and strolled back out into the second floor hallway. One of the library workers was pushing a small wooden cart loaded with books in my direction, so I swerved to the right as I passed by her. I made my way down the Italian marble stairway and back into the first floor lobby. There was a small utility door off in the left hand corner of the lobby. The door had the letters LL printed on it, which I knew stood for lower level. I opened the door, stepped inside, and quietly closed it behind me. I started down a narrow wooden staircase that was poorly lit with a single twenty-five watt light bulb. A few moments later I emerged from the stairway into a very well illuminated basement hallway. There was a green sign with red letters printed on it hanging on the wall directly in front of me. It indicated that the Research Departments was to my left and the Periodicals were to my right. I turned left and walked down the empty corridor. At the far end of the hallway was a wooden door with a frosted glass window and lettering that read *RESEARCH DEPARTMENT - EMPLOYEES ONLY!* I opened the door and strolled inside.

It was a small office with four desks lined up two by two, each of which was buried in a mound of books and paper. The news was playing on an Emerson table top AM radio that had been placed on one of the desks. All of the desks were vacant at the present time. I looked around and noticed the door to a small bathroom was closed on the opposite side of the office. I took out a cigarette, lit it up, and waited. Within a few moments a toilet flushed and I heard the sound of a faucet running inside. Finally, the door opened and a small elderly man emerged, still tucking his shirt back down inside his trousers. He was all of five feet tall and walked with a little limp. His back was hunched over a little from years of stacking and sorting through volumes of books. He was wearing a dark blue wrinkled suit with gray flannel pants that were much too big for him. He wore a green bow tie that seemed to be tied too tightly around his neck.

"Afternoon Billy!" I called out.

He looked up at me but couldn't make out my face from across the room, so he walked over to get a better look at me. A smile came over his face as he got closer "Well well, Mr. Chambers. Good afternoon to you Sir" he replied. "What brings you down to my neck of the woods on such a beautiful Sunday afternoon?" William Drum may have been in his early eighties, but he was still sharp as a tack. He had worked for the Providence Library in various capacities since it's opening in 1878 at its original location in the Butler Exchange Building. He also had a penchant for mathematics, and had helped me on numerous occasions over the years reviewing and decoding documents that needed reviewing and decoding. "Got a short letter I thought you might be able take a look at for me Billy. Not much too it really, but I was thinking maybe you would have some ideas on it?" I said as I handed the letter over to him. He lifted his reading glasses up from the lanyard hanging around his neck, and placed them over his short nose. He gave the letter a quick read and looked back up at me "Give me a few minutes and I'll see if anything sticks out at me" he said with a grin. I nodded "Perfect, I need to do a little research upstairs anyway. I'll be back down in about an hour. Thanks Pal!" I replied as I walked out of the office.

The geography section was located on the first floor of the library. When I reached the department I found a young lady seated behind the large Geography Information Desk. I approached her desk "Hey sister, could you tell me where I could find information on Mar del Plata, Buenos Aires, Argentina?" She was maybe twenty-five with deep brown eyes and Mediterranean skin. She looked me up and down for a moment and then stood up, walking out from behind the desk. "I might... follow me please" she said as she stepped in front of me and led the way down one of the narrow book aisles. She had a nice figure, one that seemed out of place in a library, and certainly didn't belong hidden behind a geography reference desk. She had long jet black hair that hung straight down over her shoulders reaching close to her waistline. It was a nice waistline. She pulled two books down from shelving a few yards apart and walked back over to me "This book should give you some good information about the country, its geography, population, commerce, politics, and climate... This other periodical is a good reference in terms of the countries culture and way of life." She paused for a moment as she handed them off to me standing barely a foot apart. "Can I do anything else for you?" she said gazing directly into my eyes. I was paralyzed for a moment or so before responding "Thanks... that should do it for now. Not to say I won't need your help a little later?" She smiled at me and let go of the books. "Sure, you know where to find me" she replied as she walked off back down the aisle. I watched her slowly walk away. I shook it off and found a small table at the end of the aisle, and sat down to catch up on Mar del Plata, Argentina.

Mar del Plata was an Argentinean city located on the Atlantic coastline two hundred and fifty miles south of Buenos Aires. It was a major fishing port and the largest seaside beach resort in Argentina. The books contained some picturesque shots of their beaches, and it looked like a nice place to vacation. Fishing, tourism, and textiles were their biggest industries, and the area had two major shipping ports. A military coup had recently placed the conservatives back into power, some thought through election fraud. The political landscape was dominated by the socialist movement, many of who had emigrated from Italy. A large casino on the waterfront had recently been built in 1939. Due to the city being a heavy destination for European tourists, the area began building many European inspired chalets during the twenties and thirties, such as the Villa Normandy. After forty-five minutes I had learned all sorts of useless tidbits about Mar del Plata, but my eyes weren't accustomed to this type of work and started to give out a little.

I closed the books and strolled back up to the girl sitting behind the reference desk. I placed the books on the desk directly in front of her. "Here you go, thanks for the help doll." She looked up and noticed the books, along with my business card wedged into one of the bindings. She smiled and looked up at me "Is there anything else I can do for you?" I smiled back and responded "Yeah, call that number when you have time. Ok?" She pulled my card out of the book and smiled "Ok."

I headed back down to the basement to see if Billy had made any progress with my letter. As I walked back into the small musty office, I noticed Billy sitting at his desk hunched over a set of old maps with a small florescent light shining down on one. He had a large square magnifying glass out and was scanning over one of the maps that was laid out directly in front of him. "Any luck with that Letter?" I said as I walked back into the room. He stood up, nodded his head a bit, and walked over to a smaller side table "A little. Care to take a look?" I nodded.

He had made a hand written copy on a separate sheet of paper, so he handed me the original letter back as we approached the table. "In general, I don't think we're dealing with any complex hidden code here" he said as he wrinkled his forehead up a little. "Although, I do think there may be a simple message hidden within the letter." I looked down at the words he had copied onto on a small piece of paper. He spread the paper out on the desk so I could see it, and pulled a pencil out from his shirt pocket. "Definitely references to several numbers in this letter. Let's look strictly at the numbers mentioned.

If you notice the first reference says that she will be staying for about ten days." He circled the word ten on the paper. "She goes on to say she passed her music test by playing Mozart's Piano Concerto number twenty-one." He circled the word twenty-one. "She then says she has three new books, which she will be bringing with her on vacation." He circled the word three. "Finally, she includes some numbers at the end of her address." He circled those numbers. I looked back at him "Yeah, I thought that was kind of strange? Maybe some sort of international telephone number or postal code?" He looked back at me "I don't think so, but I'll get to that in a second. The first two numbers seem pretty straight forward ten and twenty-one, or 10/21. My guess is that's a simple reference to October 21st. The next number is three and my first thought was that it could be a time, either 3:00am or 3:00pm. But I think the context is important here. She says she has three new books she is bringing, which he will be interested in seeing. I am guessing she is delivering three of something other than books. What is it really, who knows for sure?" He scratched his head for a moment with the end of his pencil.

"Well, what about the letters at the bottom of her address?" I asked. He glanced back over at me and smiled a little "Oh… that was easy. I would think an old navy man like you would have spotted that right away." He drew a vertical line between the last number 6 and the hyphen. I looked down at the numbers for a few seconds and then it was obvious to me. "Latitude and longitude! Right there in front of me." Billy laughed a little before replying "Yep! It has to be. Latitude positive 41.66 degrees, longitude negative 71.38 degrees. I checked the postal codes and telephone numbers in Buenos Aires, and there's nothing even close to those numbers." He leaned back and rubbed his hands together with pride. "Do you know where it is?" I asked. He turned and started back for his desk "I was working at that when you walked in young man." I followed close behind. He sat back down at his desk and lifted the magnifying glass back over a map of New England and started to scan across it. After a minute, he lifted a pencil and a ruler out from his drawer and drew a horizontal line across the map "Latitude... positive 41.6 degrees" he murmured to himself. Then he shifted the ruler and drew a vertical line down the map "longitude is negative 71.3 degrees." He lifted his head up from the map "Hmm... pretty close to home. I can't say with complete precision with this map, but it's definitely somewhere in Narragansett Bay."

He stood up and walked over to a set of shelves along the wall, which contained rolls of maps tucked away inside small cubby holes. He pulled one of the maps out from its hiding place and opened it up on the counter top. "Here's a map of just Rhode Island with latitudes and longitudes. It should be a little more exact." He bent over and pushed his reading glasses back up over his nose. "It looks to be in Greenwich Bay, maybe towards the tip of Prudence Island." I stared intently down at the map "… and Prudence Island is directly across from Warwick Point, right?" "Yes... it could be Warwick Point too." he replied. "You're the best Billy! That cinches it!" I proclaimed as I hit my closed fist on the counter top. "I owe you one Pal!" I said as I darted out of the room.

I made my way back upstairs into the main lobby, and walked out the rear doors into the parking lot. The weather had turned again and the bright sunny morning had given way to a heavy overcast afternoon with ominous low lying clouds lingering in the sky. I jumped into my car and started the engine.   The needle on my gas gauge was getting very close to empty. I checked my wallet for a couple of dollars to fill the tank. It was empty as it sometimes was, so I decided to run by the office and grab the c-note Charlotte had paid me. I knew there was a good chance that either the police or Corrao's boys would be waiting for me out front. But I had a key to the back entrance, which could hopefully get me into the building without being spotted.

A few minutes later I was pulling into my parking spot behind Miller's Grocery store. Rather than walking directly up Weybossett Street, I crossed over another block into the narrow ally that ran behind my building.   I made my way up the alley, passing dozens of overflowing trash cans along the way. I noticed a few rats getting an early start on their evening rounds, while I approached the small entrance at the rear of my building. I unlocked the steel door and started my way up the narrow cement stairway that led to the fifth floor. So far there was no sign of anyone lurking around for me. When I reached the fifth floor I turned the knob slowly, and inched the door open until I was able to peek my head through.

The corridor was empty at the moment. The main ceiling lights were turned off and only two small night lights were lit on either side of the hallway. Several beams of day light were shining through two hefty windows on either side of the corridor. I waited in the stairway for a few minutes to see if I could hear anyone inside, but there was nothing other than the banging of radiators along the wall. I walked out gingerly into the hallway and made my way down to my unit. I unlocked the door, walked inside, and strolled through the reception area into my office without turning the lights on. I walked over to the corner window and looked down onto Weybossett Street.

Traffic on the road was light, but there was a black sedan parked across the street in front of the automat. Two men in cheap suits sat in the front seat with their hats tipped down over their foreheads. It looked liked Tom had sent a couple of plain clothes officers to keep tabs on me. I laughed a little, and closed the shade down tightly. I turned back to my desk and pulled the chain on the small banker's lamp sitting on top. I sat down and pulled open the top drawer to retrieve the old cigar box. I lifted the top on the box and took out the hundred, tucking it away in my pants pocket. Then I opened a small drawer on the left side of the desk and pulled out a bottle of rye along with a shot glass. I poured myself a drink and picked up the receiver on the telephone.

It was getting late and I was getting hungry so I dialed down to Ernie's Deli on Broadway. A deep gruff voice answered the line on the other end "Ernie's." "Ernie, its Nick. Could you send up a sandwich and a coke for me? I'm in the office." I heard a lot of chatter in the background. "Sure thing Nick, I'll send Johnny over with it right away." he replied. I rubbed my forehead a little "If anyone asks who he's delivering to, just tell him to say it's for the janitor. Also, think you could break a c-note for me Ernie?" I asked. "I'll see what we have in the draw" he replied as he hung up the receiver. Ernie had the best pastrami sandwiches in the city, which was all I ever ordered. Now when I called all I needed to ask for was a sandwich and he always knew what I wanted. I poured myself another drink and eased back into my chair. I pulled the pack of Chesterfields out from my pocket, helped myself to one, and dropped the rest down on my desk.

A few minutes passed by and just as my eyes felt like closing I heard the outer door to my office creak open. It was a little too soon for Johnny to be running up with my sandwich. I leaned back in my chair and peeked out underneath the shade. The police were still on duty down below in the front seat of their parked car. Light footsteps began to approach my office door, and I could see the shadow of a figure through the frosted glass window looking out to my reception area. I leaned forward in my chair and pulled my gun out from its shoulder holster. I held the gun low behind the desk as my office door creaked open.

A small woman in her early thirties poked her head through the door "Excuse me? I am looking for Nicholas Chambers?" she asked as she took a half step into the office. She was a plain Jane. Skinny with straight dirty brown hair that was pulled back into a long pony tail. She wore tan slacks and a green turtle neck sweater with a gold pendent hanging down from her neck. She carried a small white leather purse that she held tightly in her hand. I kept my hand on my gun for the moment "Yes, that would be me, can I help you" I asked as she walked in and helped herself to the seat in front of my desk. She reached her hand out to introduce herself. I let go of the gun for a brief moment to shake her boney hand. She sat down in the easy chair, which seemed to swallow her up. "My name is Elizabeth Brennan, and I need to speak with you about Allison Baxter." She had a faint female voice, a voice I distinctly recognized as the woman who had called me early yesterday morning. I laid my gun down on my lap now, but kept my hand close by "How can I help you Miss Brennan?"

She pulled a white handkerchief out from her purse and wiped a little sweat from her brow. "I'm a little nervous to be honest Mr. Chambers, but I need to talk to you about Allison. Has she spoken with you yet?" I paused for a moment and tugged at my right earlobe "Maybe I can ask who you are first and what your interest is in all of this?" She nodded, sat up in her seat and tucked the handkerchief away in her purse "Oh yes, of course... Forgive me Mr. Chambers. I'm a friend of Allison's, and I work with her at the Journal Bulletin. She was at my house on Thursday night, and I know she was coming to see you on Friday." I shot her a perplexed look back "She was on her way to see me? Let's just slow down a bit if that's ok. Why don't you run through your story from the beginning for me." She seemed a little shaken "Ok... let me think about when it all started."

She paused for a moment and then continued on "Allison came into work a couple of weeks ago. She was acting very stressed and nervous, and at lunch I asked her what was going on. She said she had been working on a story about fish migration in Narragansett Bay, and had come across a young man who needed her help. There was a large tanker that was sailing outside of the channel and destroying his lobster pots. She actually did some research and found out that those international tankers are required to stay within the channel markers when coming up into the Port of Providence. She went down to the shipyard about two weeks ago and confronted the Captain of the ship. I know she told him that he must stay within the channel markers by law, and that she would report them to the Coast Guard if they continued. She had also discovered that this particular ship was not using a harbor pilot as soon as they entered Narragansett Bay. They were waiting until they were at least half way up the bay before calling for a pilot on the radio." I nodded "What did the captain say?" She placed her purse on my desk and put both of her puny hands up on the desktop "She said he was very irate, and threw her off the ship immediately without responding... The next day she went to her boss Mr. Thompson with the information. He told her to stay out of it, and that she should stick to the research she was assigned to. She said when she left the office that day she thought someone had followed her home, and when she came into work the next morning she felt certain some had searched through her desk.

After that she didn't come into to work for a week or so, and I didn't see her again until she showed up at my apartment on Thursday night. She was terrified and nervous, and said that two men had grabbed her when she was leaving her apartment early one morning. She had been tied up, blind folded and brought to a house where she was kept locked up in a basement for nearly a week. She said they only let her out to use the bathroom a few times a day. She had no idea who they were and why they had kidnapped her, but said she felt certain they were planning to kill her. She was somehow able to sneak out through a bathroom window one night, and flagged down a cab once she had made it out into the road." I rubbed my chin a little "Did she see anyone when she was in the house?" I asked. "She said that the only person she saw was a young woman who brought her food and let her use the bathroom. Other than that she had been blindfolded when she was moved into the house. She did say she heard male voices on occasion, but they were always speaking in some other language. She knew the house was somewhere on the East Side of Providence, but wasn't sure of the exact address because she was so disorientated when she escaped."

I could see her hand tremble a little now. "What happened when she showed up at your apartment on Thursday night? Did you call the police?" I asked. "No. I wanted to but she wouldn't let me. She wanted to get in touch with her boyfriend Johnny. She wasn't sure if it had something to do with him, and thought that maybe someone had kidnapped her to get at him. She tried to call him Thursday night but couldn't reach him, so she decided to sleep at my place. I had to go into work on Friday, but she called me in the morning to tell me she had got through to one of his employees. They were supposed to come by and pick her up around 3:00pm… She called me again around 2:00pm to let me know she was ok, and whoever she had spoken with told her that Johnny had already hired you to find her. She thought you would probably be able to help and said she was going to try and meet with you that night." She paused for a moment and became a little teary eyed. "That's the last time I spoke with her, and it's been almost two days now. Did she ever speak with you?"

I leaned back in my chair a little before responding, trying to decide if I believed her story. For some reason I did "No… I've never met Allison. I was hired by her sister… well actually by the boyfriend Johnny. I think you must have been the person who called me yesterday morning?" She nodded. "Well, unfortunately aside from that there's not much to tell." There was no good reason to trust her completely so I decided not to lay everything out for her. "Did she say anything else to you when she called? Maybe who she spoke with or who was coming to pick her up?" I questioned. She shook her head "No, just to say it was one of his employees who was coming over to get her. I'm sure you've seen some of Johnny's employees Mr. Chambers? I know those men are probably not all on the up and up, but I did think she would be safe with them." I nodded in response "I had the pleasure just last night of meeting several of them. They all seem like upstanding citizens." She rolled her eyes at me "I told her it was too dangerous to get involved with someone like that, but she wouldn't listen to me. Now look at what's happened to her. What should I do now Mr. Chambers?" she asked in a panic stricken voice. I slid the gun on my lap back down onto the seat of my chair and stood up "Nothing for now, just sit tight. You did the right thing by coming in, it's been a big help. The best thing you can do right now is to go home and get some rest. Go to work in the morning and act normal. If anyone asks, you don't know anything about anything. I'll let you know as soon as I find Allison."

Just then there were three knocks at the outside door and a voice called into the office "Ernie's, Mr. Chambers." I recognized the voice as Ernie's nephew Johnny, who did most of their deliveries. "Come in Johnny boy" I replied. "You had better be on your way now Miss Brennan. I'll be in touch as soon as I know more" I said as I shook her small hand one last time. "Thank you" she replied as she stood up and strolled out the doorway just as Johnny was walking in with my pastrami sandwich.

Johnny was about thirteen years old and maybe five

feet ten inches in height. He had a slender build and was wearing a pair of denim jeans and a dirty gray tee shirt. He walked in and dropped a brown bag on my desk. "Hey Mr. Chambers, it'll be seventy-five cents please." I handed him the hundred dollar bill. He took the bill in his hand and stared bewildered at it for almost a minute. While he admired the portrait of Benjamin Franklin, I opened the bag and unwrapped the hot pastrami sandwich. It smelled so good I immediately sunk my teeth into it.   While I was chewing, he fumbled in his pocket and pulled out a roll of nineteen five dollar bills, four ones, and a quarter. "Here's your change Mr. Chambers, Uncle Ernie already counted it out for me." I took the bills and handed him back the quarter "keep the change kid. Anyone stop you on the way up?" I questioned as I flicked the coin over my desk back at him. He caught it in mid air "Nobody, came right up on the elevator. Thanks for the tip!" he replied as he abruptly darted out of the office. Kids always seemed to be in a hurry for one reason or another. I ate my sandwich and enjoyed every minute of it. I pulled the bottle of coke out from the brown bag and popped the cap off using the metal edge of my desktop. I started to drink it down and thought about the case.

It was just starting to get dark outside, so I turned the light off in my office because I didn't want to tip off the police on watch down below. I took a quick look out the window to make sure they were still there, and they were. I got up and lingered over to a small couch I kept in the office for moments like this. I fell onto the couch and let my head rest comfortably on the end pillow. I let my eyes close, fell asleep and dreamt about lobsters, Argentine beaches, and pretty librarians.

16: Monday Morning

I awoke to the sound of a loud obnoxious horn blaring on the street outside of my building. I eased open my tired eyes and saw two beams of dust filled sunlight streaking across my office from the filthy window on the far side of the room. As I started to wake up, I could hear more sounds of traffic passing down on the street below. It was Monday morning and people were on their way into work now. I looked up at the old wooden cuckoo clock hanging above the sideboard, which showed the time to be half past seven in the morning. The cuckoo had stopped working several years ago, but the clock still kept good time. I could hear a trolley banging by and ringing its bell as it passed the corner intersection. Two men were shouting something at each other in Portuguese, while a newspaper boy was selling papers for a nickel each. I sat up in the couch and let my head get its balance back. I walked over to the sink and splashed a little water in my face, then strolled to the window and snapped open the shade. The street was alive again with cars and pedestrians. My friends in the black sedan were still parked across the street. One of the officers was standing outside now, leaning up against the car and smoking a cigarette. The weather had not improved much since last night as clouds filled a gray overcast sky. It wasn't raining yet, but it looked as though it could let go at any minute.

I moved away from the window and walked slowly back over to my desk. I picked up the half smoked pack of Chesterfields from my desk, pulled out a cigarette, lit it and took a deep drag. There was usually nothing like a good smoke first thing in the morning. But I had a splitting headache from smoking these tasteless cigarettes, and needed to get over to the pharmacy for more aspirin and a pack of Lucky Strike. I couldn't stand Chesterfield, but smoking nothing would be even worse on my poor head. Just then the telephone on my desk rang and I lifted the receiver "Hello, Nicholas Chambers". A gruff voice that I recognized came over the line "Nick, its Tom. We might have found you're missing person. Take a walk over to the corner of Union & Worchester Street. It's only a few blocks from your office." He hung up the phone abruptly before I could say anything. I dropped my gun into my desk for safekeeping, grabbed my hat and jacket, and flew out through my office door. I ran through my reception area and out into the hallway, slamming the door behind me.

The fifth floor hallway looked much different than it had just the night before. It was buzzing with people darting from office to office, and the elevators were working hard transporting workers up and down between floors. A young woman was pushing a small wooden cart loaded with stacks of typewriter paper, while an older biddy gabbed away in her ear about their boss's transgressions. Two aging well dressed men in gray pinstriped suits stood on the far end of the corridor smoking cigarettes and discussing the day's business. I darted into an open door on one of the elevators and pushed the lobby button. The elevator doors closed and it began moving up, and I started cursing at myself for not taking the stairs. Five stops later, I stepped out into the first floor of the building and hastily walked across the spacious black tiled lobby out onto Weybosett Street. The doorman's name was Charlie and he caught a glimpse of me coming out of the building "Heading the wrong way aren't you Mr. Chambers?" he joked with a little laughter. I nodded back "I think you're right Chuck." I jogged through heavy traffic across the street, and walked up the sidewalk to the black sedan, which was still parked where it had been the night before. I stuck my head in through the window "How about ride fellas? Your boss is a few blocks over looking for me?" They both turned at me, eyes fuming, and looking quite irritated "Get in the back Chambers" one of them ordered.

I opened the back door and slid into the seat. They both sat up straight and rubbed their eyes a little. It had apparently been a long unproductive night. I heard some keys jingle and then the engine turned over. "Detective Bradley just called, needs me over at the corner of Union & Worchester, pronto" I instructed. They both turned back over the seat and shot me annoyed expressions as we started down the street. Three blocks later we were pulling up to a scene with several police cars and the coroner's wagon. A police officer stood in the center of the road, turning back any oncoming traffic. As we approached our driver stuck his head out of the window and shouted something to the officer. The cop nodded and waived us on through. We parked directly behind the coroner's truck, which was parked a little further up Union St. One of the men turned back at me "Don't move!" he commanded as he and the other officer exited the vehicle. They walked behind the car and crossed over onto Union St, and then walked out of sight onto Worchester, which was more of a back alley.   About ten minutes passed before one of the men returned out from the alley and approached the car. He opened the back door to let me out "Follow me Chambers!" I stepped out of the vehicle and closed the door behind me.

He walked in front of me and led me back into the dingy alley. There were several plain clothes officers standing about twenty yards ahead of us in front of a basement stairwell talking to one another. One of the officers was Detective Bradley. He motioned to me as I approached "Pretty grisly one Nick. Ok if you take a look to see if she's your missing person?" "Sure, she's down there?" I replied.   "Yeah, let's take a look" he said as he began walking down the stairwell. As I came to the top of the cement stairway, I immediately noticed the body of a young women lying at the base of the stairs. Her long brown hair was soaking in a pool of dark brown blood, and the shirt she was wearing was drenched in it. Halfway down the stairs Tom stopped and pointed out some dried blood and hair stuck to the cement wall leading down "Looks like she hit her head here on the way down." He continued down to the base of the stairs and stepped off to one side of the body. I stood on the opposite side. Her face was looking straight up at me, eyes wide open. She was in her early twenties, slim, had a dark complexion and was wearing a half wool jacket with short sleeves. She had on an unbuttoned blue cardigan sweater with a pleated gray skirt that ran down to her knees. Her white button down shirt with a peter pan collar was completely drenched in blood. A small black purse was still clenched in her hand.   "Well, what do think Nick?" Tom questioned.

I pulled out the photo of Allison from my jacket pocket and took a good look at it. It didn't take very long "Yeah, that's her alright. Her name's Allison Baxter. How long you figure she's been down here for?" I asked. He bent down on one knee to get a closer look "The M.E. already gave her the once over. Right now he's saying about two days, maybe three. He'll know more when he gets her back on the table." Tom pulled out two cigarettes, lit one for me and handed it over. "How about a cause of death?" I asked. He pushed her over on one side and pulled her shirt up revealing a two inch hole in her lower back. "She definitely had some head trauma, but she's got this stab wound in her lower right back... looks like it went right through one of her Kidneys." He took a pencil out and opened the wound somewhat, revealing the organ inside. "Yeah, that's ok Tom... I don't need an anatomy lesson right now, anything else?" I questioned. He flipped her over again flat on her back and lifted the blood stained shirt up from her stomach. I could see multiple stab wounds spread across her abdomen. "The M.E. counted five separate stab wounds in her gut. Our best guess right now is that she was stabbed from behind at the top of the stairway, and then fell down the stairs, cracking her head on the cement wall. We think she landed on her back and the murderer followed her down to give her five more in the gut... Make sense?" he asked. I took another good look at her "Yeah, fits pretty well. Why else would she have stab wounds on both sides of her body? How about a murder weapon?"

Tom stood back up and walked over to a small ledge in the corner of the stairwell. He lifted a large kitchen knife up and handed it to me. The white bone handle was hard to make out through the dried blood. The stainless steel blade was a good ten inches in length and its width was at least 3 inches at the base. "Left right beside the body, and it matches up with the wounds perfectly." he replied. "Although, it looks like it's been wiped clean for prints." I rubbed the back of my neck and took a deep breath "Is that all of it?" "That's it" he replied "Unless you see something else?" I looked around the area one last time "Not much. Her purse is still in her hand, so I doubt if we're talking robbery here." Tom nodded "Agreed, we checked the purse and her driver's license and three dollars were still tucked away inside." We both turned and started up the stairs.

When we cleared the top, the Coroner was rolling a stretcher up to us. "All set now Detective" he questioned. Tom looked over at him "All yours Bill. I'll be down to see you later once you've had a chance to take a better look at her." He and another officer started to carry the stretcher down the stairway. I finished my cigarette and tossed it into the gutter "OK Pal, well I guess I'll catch up with you later." Tom turned quickly back towards me "Hold on a second Nick!" He motioned to an enormous officer standing guard in the alley. "You need to come down to the station and speak with the Captain, and it needs to be now." I looked at the large officer who had already pulled a set of handcuffs from his belt. "Tom, I won't get anywhere if I'm hung up down at the station answering ridiculous questions from the old man?" He gestured to the oversized officer "Bring him back to the station and put him on ice until the Captain is ready to talk with him." Before I could speak again the giant had shoved my face into the wall and was handcuffing my hands behind my back. "Really Tom? Handcuffs? Were all adults here?" He just shook his head "Take him back" he said as the officer grabbed me by the shoulder and brought me back out to Union St.

A quick ride in a squad car had me back at the Providence Police Station, and within a few minutes I was being escorted down a short corridor on the first floor. The short hallway had several narrow doors with small barred windows. The guard pulled some keys from his pocket and opened the steel plated door. "Here you go Dick" he said motioning for me to step inside. "It's Nick" I replied as I entered the small cell. "Whatever you say Dick. Settle in... It could be a while" he replied as he removed the cuffs from my wrists and then slammed the door closed. I heard the locking mechanism latch inside the door and footsteps started clicking away up the tiled corridor.

There was a fold up metal bed along one of the walls that I folded down. A small faucet stood in the corner of the room, and a clean blanket and pillow sat on top of a painted shelf just above the sink. I grabbed both and sat down on the thin bumpy mattress. I lied back on the bed resting my exhausted back, closed my eyes and tried to get some overdue rest. Around noontime the door opened and an officer walked inside to deliver a small tray of food. It contained a glass of water, two slices of bread with butter, and a small cup of chicken noodle soup. I was extremely famished so I ate everything on the plate and placed the empty tray on the floor. I sat down on the lumpy bed again and thought about what and how much I should say to the captain if they ever brought me upstairs.

About three hours later I heard footsteps approaching my cell, and someone began unlocking the door on the outside. Suddenly the door creaked open and the same smartass officer was standing just outside the doorway. "Follow me!" was all he said as he turned and walked back down the corridor. I wasn't arguing so I picked up my hat and coat and skipped out behind him. He led me down the hallway and back out into the main lobby in front of the elevators. I asked if we could take the stairs, but he just growled back at me. One elevator arrived and opened its doors for us. We decided to enter, and once we were aboard he pushed the button for the fourth floor. As the doors closed we began to move up, and I suddenly felt a little claustrophobic. We heard several very load bangs on the way up, and I could swear I smelled something burning. When we reached the fourth floor, the lift settled into place and the brass doors rolled open. I jumped out quickly, thinking the car might plummet to the bottom at any moment.

The fourth floor was a very quiet place compared to the rest of the station. I hadn't been up there much and when I did it was never under good circumstances. My escort walked me down the hallway and knocked on the third door to the left. The gold plaque on the door with black lettering read "Capt. Eugene Baxter, Police Chief." Someone inside shouted out for us to enter, and the officer turned the brass knob and pushed the door open. "Here he is Chief" he said as he stood aside and motioned me into the room.   As I walked into the spacious room, I saw the Captain standing behind an oversized Mahogany desk with a brass banker's lamp sitting on top. Two other men stood next to his desk in plain clothes looking interested in what I might have to say. Tom was seated directly in from of the Captain's desk, and there was an empty seat aside of him. "Have a seat Chambers" the Captain said as he motioned for me to sit next to Tom.

The Captain was an elderly man in his early seventies, but still had most of his wits about him. He was tall and lanky, maybe six feet three inches in height.   He was bald with some leftover gray hair still clinging to life on either side of his head. He wore white trousers, and a white button up cotton shirt with a captain's shield stuck to it. There was a dress white hat sitting on his desktop, which looked like it didn't get much wear. He stood up behind the desk in front of his large worn-out leather chair.

"Let me start off by saying that we have two dead women here Chambers, both of whom were acquainted with you. Both have clearly been murdered, and you are the only link we have between them. So I suggest you lay it all out for us now, and don't keep anything to yourself." He paused for a few seconds and then continued on. "If I think for one moment you haven't been one thousand percent honest with us, I'll pull your license and put you on a wagon up to the state prison, where you can pass the months waiting for your case to go to trial. Do we understand each other?" he asked. I looked up from my seat at him "Alright Captain, I'll tell you what I know." He sat down "You had better hope its good enough!"

I placed my hat down on his desk, and stood up to remove my overcoat. I draped it over the back of the chair and sat back down. "Got a call on Friday from a woman claiming to be Allison's sister Jill. She came by my office around 5:00pm and hired me to find her. I got shanghaied leaving my office that night and was brought out to an old bungalow down on Warwick Neck. The house had a 1939 black DeSoto in the garage, and I saw two men coming in from the ocean on a small powerboat. I got sapped down at that point, but managed to escape later and made my way back home. I can tell you this gang definitely meant business." The Captain interrupted me "what kind of racket were they running?" I pulled the pack of Chesterfield's out from my pocket and tapped a cigarette out. There was a large lead crystal lighter on his desk that I helped myself to. "Can't say for sure yet, but whatever it is, it involves a foreign tanker that has been making unscheduled stops just off the coast on Warwick Point. A local lobsterman by the name Billy Gibson had a run in with them a few weeks ago, and he just washed up dead on the beach Saturday morning. Police are saying it was a fishing accident? My client ends up dead the same day, dumped behind an old warehouse down by the shipyard with two slugs to the side of her head. Allison, the missing person, had been doing some research for the Journal on fish migration in Greenwich Bay. She had interviewed Billy Gibson a week earlier, and he happened to tell her about his run in with the tanker. So she starts poking around for him as reporters usually do. She was the blood drenched girl you pulled out of the alley stairwell early this morning. Someone had used her stomach as a pin cushion for their kitchen knife."

I paused and took another drag on my cigarette before continuing on. "I asked Detective Bradley to meet me out at the house on Warwick Neck yesterday, but they had already cleared out by the time we got there." I looked over and noticed that one of the men standing off to the side had been keeping notes on everything I said. The Captain stared across the desk at me "What was the name of the Tanker?" I scratched the back of my neck a bit, trying to decide if I knew the answer. I decided I did. "The Argentine Mist, she was still tied up down in the Providence Pier last time I checked."

The old man piped up again "Could be bootlegging. We repealed Prohibition back in thirty-three, but you still have these crazy bootleggers trying to avoid the state and federal taxes. There used to be a lot of rum runners out off Warwick Neck in the twenties and thirties, bringing in rum from the Caribbean. Could be someone decided to kick start the old business again." He looked over at Tom "Let's do some background work on this ship Tom. Contact the Harbor Master, Coast Guard if needed. Let's see what we can turn up." Tom nodded "Will do Captain." He turned back towards me "What do you think Chambers, Bootleggers?" he questioned. I knew the old timer had spent his glory days chasing rum runners down during prohibition, but I was pretty sure these weren't bootleggers. I nodded my head anyway "Makes as much sense as anything Captain, but I just can't say for sure right now." He picked up a pencil from his desk and began scribbling something on a small pad "What else Chambers?" I took one last drag on my cigarette, sat up in my seat, and put it out using the glass ashtray on the edge of his desk "Well that's everything Captain. Like I said, I've only been on this a couple of days." He let out an exasperated sigh and shook his head a little. "You said you were hired by someone who claimed to be Allison's sister. Is there some reason you think she wasn't?" "No, not really... But now that I've had a chance to see Allison, I just don't see the family resemblance. My clients aren't always one hundred percent honest with me" I replied. He looked back over to Tom "What do you think Tom?" Tom shot a quick glance at me and then turned back towards his captain "Nick's always been pretty upfront with us Sir. No reason to think he's not on the level now."

The Captain stood up "We'll... you better hope you've been one hundred percent honest with me Chambers. If I find out otherwise, you'll be spending the holidays in a six by eight cell as a guest of the state. Understood?" he questioned. I nodded. "You can leave now, but we may need you for more questioning so stay close to your phone." I stood up "Yes Sir" I replied as I began walking out of the room. "Hold up a second Nick" Tom called out as he followed me out into the hallway.

"I stuck my neck out for you in there pal, so you had better call me the second anything turns up, got it?" I put my overcoat on, twirled my hat and replied "I got you Tom, as soon as I know something you'll be the first one I call." I said goodbye and walked down the corridor to the stairway.

I headed down the stairs and thought about how much I had told the Captain. Everything was true for the most part, but I had left out Corrao and Strauss. I didn't mention Corrao because it just wasn't good business for a PI to admit to the police he's working for a mob boss, and it was never smart from a health standpoint to give up a mob boss to the cops. I left out Strauss and the house on the East Side because I didn't want the cops mussing over there before I had a chance to get back out and find some real evidence. They had already cleared out of the Warwick Neck property, and I knew at best I had a few hours before they would do the same up on the East Side.

I left the station and started walking back to my car, which was still parked four blocks away behind Miller's. It was a little after 6:00pm now, and a light drizzle had begun to fall down on the city. The streets were bustling with people on their way home from work. What I had in mind needed to wait until nightfall, and I was getting pretty hungry in the meantime. I decided to stop in at the Empire Street Pharmacy to get a quick sandwich and maybe a little aspirin.

A gold brass bell hanging above the entrance rang as I stepped through the front door into the pharmacy. One side of the store had rows of shelving stocked with everything from soap to baking soda. Off to the right was a soda fountain with a three patrons seated at it. In the far corner of the store was the pharmacy counter, where sick people picked up pills to dull their pain. I walked across the worn out tiled floor and took a seat at the counter. Within a few minutes a young women in her early thirties wearing a dark blue sweater and a white cotton jump skirt emerged from the back. She filled the sweater nicely, wore black lace stockings and had auburn hair that was feathered out on both sides. The red head walked over to the counter in front of me to take my order. "What can I get you mister?" she asked. I took my hat off and placed it down on the empty counter. "How about an egg sandwich and some fries?" She pulled out a small pad and jotted my order down "Something to drink with that?" I looked back up at her "I'll take a coke, and you can add a couple of aspirin to that sister. I've got a splitting headache that I need to tone down." She finished scribbling on her pad, nodded and walked off.

I pulled out what was left of my cigarettes, lit one up, and glanced around to take a quick inventory. There was an overweight older woman with white greasy hair sitting three stools down on the left from me. She was eating a slice of apple pie with vanilla ice cream that she clearly could do without. A boring well dressed businessman in his forties sat two stools down to my right, drinking his lunch out of a shot glass. A young girl in her teens with bad teeth sucked on a root beer float at the end of the counter. The store itself was mostly empty, aside from a little old man waiting in front of the pharmacy counter for his medicine.

Five minutes later the waitress reappeared with my sandwich and fries. She placed the food down in front of me and grabbed a glass from above the counter. She walked to the soda fountain and worked the stainless steel lever on the unit labeled Coca Cola. She let the head settle a bit before bringing the glass over to me, and dropped two aspirin next to it on the countertop. Fifteen minutes later everything was gone, and I was smoking my last cigarette. The red head came by again to ask if I needed anything more. I told her I needed a pack of Luck Strike, so she walked off to find one for me. A minute later she came back with a pack of Chesterfields in her hand "All out of Lucky's right now, how about Chesterfield?" she questioned. I didn't know what was going on with the Chesterfields, other than they tasted like crap, but I took them anyway. "Thanks sister" I replied as I tucked the pack away I my pocket. She dropped the check down in front of me, which came to a buck ten. I left a dollar twenty and walked back out onto Empire Street.

The streets were beginning to quiet down now, and the rain had picked up a little. It was just after seven, and darkness had begun to envelop the city streets. I walked a few blocks back to Millers Grocery, and jumped into my car. I started the engine up and headed for the East Side. I needed to get back into that house and I wanted a better look in that writing desk.

By 7:30pm I was driving up Blackstone Blvd, and passed by the large Tudor at two hundred and ten. I turned down the side street that abutted the north side of the property, and pulled my car up under the shady oak tree I had used to scale the wall just a day earlier. I turned the engine off, reached over to my glove compartment, and pulled out the

Hammer's gun along with the small pen flashlight I kept inside.   I stepped out of my car, tucked the gat in my jacket, locked the door and walked around to the high brick wall encircling the property.   I jumped up onto my rear bumper and grabbed a hold of a small overhanging branch, which I used to lift myself up and over the top of the wall.

I landed hard on the other side, and crawled back up to the dividing wall that ran across the back yard.   I stood up and peered over the top of the wall.   The main house was completely quiet, and there were no lights at all on the first floor. I noticed a small lamp turned on in one of the upstairs bedroom. The gate house was lit up, and just as I was looking in that direction the gardener stepped outside for a minute to take some garbage out. He tossed the bag into a can and then stopped to light up a cigarette. I stayed down low, and let him enjoy his smoke. After a few minutes he tossed the butt to the ground and walked back into his miniature house. I kept low and made my way along the retaining wall, working across the back yard as I had done the day before.   I reached the other side, climbed up over the half wall, and ran across the lawn to the back door of the garage. I turned the knob, which was still open and stepped into a pitch black garage.

It took a minute for my eyes to adjust, but soon objects came into focus. The Cadillac and the Olds were still parked where they had been yesterday, but the first garage was empty now and the DeSoto was missing. I pulled the penlight out of my pocket, clicked the small bulb on and took a look around. There was a set of stairs on the far end of the garage that led to a side door of the main house. I climbed up the stairs and quietly turned at the door knob, but it was locked. Just then I noticed a rickety wooden stairway at the back of the garage leading up to an overhead loft, and decided to give it a go.

The first step creaked a little as I put my weight on it. The stairway was coated in a layer of dust and looked as though it hadn't been climbed in years. I made my way slowly up the stairs and stepped into a dusty loft. The room smelled old and musty, and there were several wooden crates stacked along the left wall. Stacks of forgotten newspapers lined the side of the loft. Some were dated from 1918 and reported on the Spanish Flu epidemic in Providence. At the far end of the loft was a half door locked with a small hook and eye latch. I walked over, unlatched it, and pulled the tiny door open.

It was completely black inside, so I pointed my pen light into the darkness. It illuminated a three foot high passage way running about twenty feet along the inside of the roofline. There was another door on the opposite end of the small crawl space. This looked like my way into the house, so I got down on my knees and started crawling across towards the other side.

The passageway was damp and musty, and smelled like an attic that hadn't been opened in years. I pushed through walls of cob webs as I made my way across the cramped space. When I reached the other side I pushed open the half door and crawled into a large walk-in closet. I detected a vague smell of moth balls. There was nothing but darkness inside aside from the narrow beam coming from my small pen light. I stood up in the closet and took a good look around without moving. It appeared to be a man's closet, with half a dozen pressed suits hanging neatly along one side. There were at least two dozen ties lining the inside of an open chest of drawers. The chest had two decorative cabinets on each side and three ordinary looking unfinished oak drawers below. I walked over to the closet door, and stood still for a moment to listen, but everything was silent on the opposite side.

I turned the brass door knob, pushed open the door, and peered into a large bedroom with twenty-foot plaster ceilings. A dim light from the hallway shinned into the bedroom, so I turned my pen light off. There was a very large four poster mahogany bed protruding out from one of the walls. A large green Victorian lamp hung from the center of the ceiling, and an immense mirror with decorative gold leaf along its border was bolted on the wall opposite the bed. Two enormous floor-to-ceiling windows stood on either side of the mirror, and looked out on what I assumed were the back yard and the Blackstone River. I walked over to the door leading out to the hallway, and poked my head through the opening into the upstairs hallway.

It was a long wide hallway with polished parquet flooring that ran sixty to seventy feet along the expanse of the second floor. I paused again to listen for any sounds, but still only heard silence. A light was peering out under the door of a bedroom at the far end of the hallway.   I noticed two stairways on either side of the hallway.   They were the same two staircases I had seen on my last visit to the house. They rolled down the side walls of the home and met at a platform halfway down. There was a central stairway at that point leading down into the front hall.   I made my way gingerly down the wooden staircase onto the middle platform and paused again to listen. After a few seconds of nothing, I started slowly down the central stairway, stepping onto the marble floor of the front hall. I quickly moved inside the same library I had been a guest in the day before.

I closed the door quietly behind me as I entered the room. The only light now in the study was the moonlight shining through the bay windows on the opposite side of the room. I pulled my pen light out again and headed straight for the writing desk. The key was still in the candy dish on top. I picked it up and slid the tiny skeleton key into the lock, turned it, and dropped the desk cover down.

The stack of correspondence was still neatly placed off to the left side. I picked up the pile of letters, and shined my pen light on them. There were dozens of letters addressed from dozens of people with addresses all over the United States. I stuffed the letters into my jacket pocket, and pulled open the left drawer. The clip was gone and the drawer was completely empty now. I pulled at the second drawer on the right, but it was still locked as tight as it had been the day before. I picked up a large stainless steel letter opener with a black ivory handle and jammed it into the lid of the drawer. It took a little muscle, but it finally popped open. I stopped for a moment because I thought I had heard something moving overhead. After a minute of silence, I pulled the drawer completely open.

There was a lot of the typical junk you always find in junk drawers. But there was one item that caught my eye, which you typically don't find in the everyday junk drawer. It was a small round lapel pin about the size of a quarter. I picked it up and pointed my pen light down onto it. It had red lettering around an outer blue rim which read National-Sozialistiche-D.A.P. Offhand, I wasn't sure what that meant, but I was sure what the symbol in the center meant. The center circle was solid white with a black symbol that was unmistakable to me or anyone who had seen a newsreel over the past year. The swastika was the tainted good luck symbol being used to death by those socialist monkeys over in Germany, and the fact that Strauss had a Nazi membership pin sitting in his drawer made me wonder what I had walked into. I tucked the pin away in my pants pocket and closed the desk cover. I locked it back up and left the key where I had found it. I had what I came for, and some of the pieces to this case where starting to add up in my head. I just needed to make a phone call to the police, and let them blow in and round up these monkeys.

As I started to walk out of the study, I noticed a panel next to the fireplace that seemed a little out of place. I walked closer and noticed a one inch gap between the paneling and the stone fireplace. I pulled the paneling to the left and it slide open easily as if it were on rollers. The opening revealed a narrow passageway about two feet wide that wound its way behind the fireplace. I stepped inside, slide the panel closed behind me, and was suddenly enveloped by blackness. I clicked on my trusty pen light, which was starting to dim a little at this point, and headed down the narrow passageway. It wound around the back of the fireplace until it reached a small stairway that appeared to lead down into the basement. I headed down the steep set of steps and opened a door at the base of the stairway. It led to a small dimly lit stale flavored room. There were cement walls on all sides of the room, and the door I had entered through seemed to be the only entrance and exit.

In the dark I could make out a small table with a chair setup along one of the Walls. I pulled on a chain hanging from the ceiling in the center of the room, and a light bulb switched on overhead. Things became clearer once my eyes adjusted to the light. A small short wave radio sat on top of the table, and the cable that came out of it reached up through a small basement window. The radio had three different dials, several indicator lights, and a microphone that was latched on to its side. We had used similar units in the Navy, which had a range of about fifty miles. Stacks of unused photo paper were neatly piled on a shelf above the table, and looked very similar to the paper the cops had found on Warwick Neck. There was also a small tin box on the shelf that I pulled down. I placed the box on the table and opened it. It contained about twenty blank U.S. Passports, a pen and an ink blotter. I looked around the room again and noticed what appeared to be a small camera mounted to a tripod on one side of the room. Things were starting to add up nicely.

Just then I heard the door behind me creak open. I spun around and saw Strauss standing in the doorway holding something in his hand. The something looked to be a Luger P08, and my guess was it contained the missing clip from the writing desk. "Good evening Mr. Chambers. What an unexpected surprise to see you here again." He stepped a little closer to me.   "Yes, we know your real name!   Nicholas Chambers, Private Investigator. You were hired to find a particularly meddlesome young woman named Allison Baxter who has been missing for the past week. It's such a shame that no one will care enough to hire someone to find you when you go missing later tonight." I decided to let that slide and shot him an indifferent glance back without saying anything. He motioned with his gun "If you wouldn't mind handing your weapon over to me, handle first if you please." I reached inside my jacket and he quickly cocked back the action on his weapon. I slowly lifted the gun out, but first, from my jacket pocket and handed it over to him. He took it with his left hand and dropped it into the side pocket of the lush bathrobe he was wearing.

Just then two other men came barreling down the stairs and barged into the small room, both carrying guns. A shorter soiled man held a Luger similar to the gun Strauss was carrying, while a second enormous man was carrying a .45 Thompson submachine gun. "Take him back upstairs into the library and secure him" Strauss ordered. The larger thug with the Tommy gun got behind me and jammed the muzzle into my spine "Move!" he shouted. As I passed by Strauss, he stuck his arm out in front of my chest motioning for me to stop "Just one moment Mr. Chambers, I'll have those letters please." I reached into my left jacket pocket, pulled out the correspondence, and handed it over to him. The thug behind me immediately slammed his elbow on the back of my shoulder, giving me an overly friendly push through the doorway. I could hear Strauss firing up the radio as we walked back up the stairway. We made our way back up to the first floor and stepped into the study.

The second gunsel was already waiting for me with some rope and a chair. The large thug reminded me that he was holding a Tommy gun by striking the back of my neck with its wooden handle. It dazed me as dropped to the ground. I felt someone pick me up and sit me down in the chair. After a minute or so, things started to come back into focus. My hands had been tied tightly to the rear chair legs behind my back. The barrel of the Tommy gun was pointed directly at my head while the giant man holding it stood directly in front of me. The smaller man with the pistol finished tying me up and then abruptly left the room. About ten minutes passed while the large goon stood silently in over me with his arms folded, pointing the barrel at my face.

Strauss finally emerged from the basement room. He brushed some dust from his bathrobe, and shot an irritated look at me. He turned to the thug guarding me. "We have our orders, execute Herunterfahren!" and then stormed out of the room without saying anything further to me. I looked up at the thug and quipped "Well, I'm glad my name isn't Herunterfahren." He wasn't laughing and took a step closer to me. He was wearing a sleeveless wife beater tee shirt, and he had a large tattoo of a black eagle on his shoulder. He slammed the gun handle violently upside my head. The room began spinning again.

It took maybe fifteen minutes for the room to stop moving. It was just about that time that Strauss walked back into the library. He had changed and was now dressed in tan slacks, a black turtle neck sweater, and a long black trench coat. He was carrying a brief case under one arm, and I noticed the Luger tucked away in a leather shoulder holster. He held a brown felt hat with black trim under his other hand. "Well Mr. Chambers. It looks like this is goodbye for us... or at least for you. I'm sorry you felt the need to keep prying into our affairs, but unfortunately this isn't going to end pleasantly for you." he said with zero emotion. I looked back up at him "So what's your racket Strauss? Helping friends of the fatherland settle into the U.S.? That house out on Warwick Neck is just a drop off point, or are you keeping tabs on the Navy operating down at Quonset Point? Maybe radioing their activity back to your axis buddies? Either way you're playing for the wrong team in my book Strauss." He smiled at me and rubbed his narrow chin a little "Well, I can't say I'm familiar with your book Mr. Chambers, but I assure you I am playing for the right team. You have no idea how committed our people are to our movement. You lazy Americans are sleeping while the rest of the world transforms itself into a new order. You go out to your movies and drink your Coca-Cola and soda pop, while we fight a war that will create a glorious new society for all the people of the world."

I shook my head and laughed a little "Tell that to the Czechs you muscled over, and the Poles you bombed into submission in thirty-nine." It was at that point that I began to detect the strong odor of gasoline fumes seeping into the room. I looked out into the hallway and saw the smaller man pouring gasoline from a metal tank onto the floor and stairway. Strauss put his hat on his head "Someday Mr. Chambers, people like you will understand our level of commitment, and the fact that resistance to our movement is futile. Enjoy your last few moments by the fire." He turned to the large goon guarding me "Make certain he is unable to leave Max, and then follow us to the ship in the Oldsmobile". He turned and walked calmly out of the room.

Two men and the young lady I had seen yesterday joined him in the hallway. They spoke for a brief moment and walked off. I heard the front door open, followed by the distinct sound of a lighter flipping open and a roller striking flint. Suddenly a silver plated lighter engulfed in flames sailed through the air onto the floor. Within seconds the front hallway burst into orange and blue flames. I looked up at the large goon who was still guarding me just as a big smile came over his face. He put the Tommy gun down on a side table, and walked closer to me while rolling up his sleeves and clenching his enormous fists. He apparently hadn't beaten me enough, and needed one more shot at me before taking off with his friends. He cocked his large arm back and took a good roundhouse swing at my head. As he did, I shifted my weight and fell over sideways onto the floor, barely ducking under his powerful punch.

I laughed at him "Not much of a fighter, are you Max?" I quipped. He became visibly enraged and stormed towards me. He reached down and grabbed my throat with one hand and the base of the chair with his other hand. He lifted both of us up over his chest, grunted loudly, and hurled us into the stone fireplace. We hit hard, and fell like a rock to the ground. The chair shattered on impact. My left hand was completely free now, while the right hand was still tied to a splintered chair leg. I staggered to my feet, and tried to get my bearings. He screamed something incoherently at me in a language I didn't understand and charged violently in my direction. My survival instincts took over, and just as he was about to grab my neck I thrust the splintered chair leg directly into his abdomen. This only seemed to anger him more. He grabbed my neck again, pinned me up against the stone fireplace, and began to strangle me with his massive hands. My face began to turn purple as I pulled the splintered wood out of his abdomen and thrust it into another area of his stomach. I think I heard him groan a little more with my second effort. I began to get dizzy and the room was starting to darken a little, so I made one last attempt.   I pulled the makeshift knife out from his abdomen, and gave a roundhouse action with my arm, landing the piece of wood several inches into the side of his throat. Blood gushed out, squirting onto my face. He stood still gazing eye to eye with me for a moment, and then I felt his grip on my neck begin to relax. Suddenly, he dropped backward like a rock slamming to the floor, never closing his eyes.

I coughed and gagged, catching my breath for a moment. I looked up and the flames had engulfed the doorway to the front hall, and the bookshelves in the library had already fallen victim. I moved quickly over to the small side table and grabbed the Tommy Gun, throwing the leather strap over my shoulder.   I ran to the back of the study and picked up a small oriental throw rug lying in front of the writing desk.   I took a few steps back and charged towards the large bay window overlooking the back yard. I plunged through the window panes, shielding myself with the rug. I fell a good ten feet onto the grass and landed hard.

I lied on the damp grass for a few minutes trying to catch my breath. It was raining pretty hard now, and I heard a load thunder echoing in the distance. Flames were pouring out of the window just ten feet over me. As I was lying on the wet ground, I heard the sound of a boat engine turn over in the direction of the Blackstone River. I lifted my head to look down in that direction and saw a small motor boat take off on the river with four passengers. It was heading for Narragansett Bay and the Port of Providence. I sat up in the rain and untied what was left of the wooden chair leg from my arm. A second later I stood up and ran across the expansive well groomed lawn towards the exterior wall. I turned to look back at the large Tudor estate, which was now completely engulfed in flames.

In a few minutes I had scaled the wall and was back sitting in my car out of the rain. Neighbors had already begun gathering out on Blackstone Boulevard, and I only had minutes before the police and fire engines arrived. I dropped the Tommy gun on the front seat of my car, started the engine and sped off. I swerved onto Blackstone Blvd and gunned the engine. The one thing I didn't need right now was to get stopped by the cops with a machine gun sitting on my front seat. After a few minutes I slowed down, turned the car onto Gano Street, and headed in the direction of the

Providence Shipyard.

Five minutes later I was driving down Allens Ave just outside of the Shipyard. I switched my lights off as I headed down Terminal Street. Half way down I turned my engine off and coasted into a spot behind a small shipping warehouse, which was maybe a hundred yards down from Pier 2. I had forgotten to stop for gas, and I noticed my fuel gauge was on empty now.

I grabbed the Tommy gun from the front seat and pulled out the clip to check for ammo. The magazine was full, so I snapped it back into the muzzle and threw the leather strap back over my shoulder. I stepped out of the car and crossed over Terminal Street, making my way along the shoreline in the direction of Pier 2. The wind and rain had picked up along the water now and was beating against me with a pretty heavy force. It took me about five minutes, but I made it over to the edge of Pier 2 and crouched down next to the door of a small receiving office. I glanced through one of the dirty window panes in the door, and noticed a black phone atop a small dispatch desk. I opened one of the window panes with the heel of my gun, and reached inside to unlock the door. I walked into the small office and picked up the telephone receiver, dialed the police station, and asked for Detective Bradley. He was unavailable, so I decided to leave an urgent message with the night sergeant. I hung up the telephone, opened the door, and walked back outside into the downpour. I knelt down and took a position at the end of the pier behind some crates.

Unlike the last time I had seen her, the Argentine Mist's was buzzing with activity. Bright lights blanketed the deck of the ship, as dozens of weary looking crew members hurried back and forth preparing for her departure. Black smoke was pouring out of her engine stacks. I glanced down towards the water and saw a small motor boat tied to a dock about half way down the pier. It was the same small boat that I had seen leave Strauss's place on the East Side a few minutes earlier. The boat was empty now, and I was pretty sure they had already made their way back onto the Mist. Two large men stood guard at the boarding ramp leading up to the ship's deck. No guns were visible but I wasn't laying bets they were empty handed. I picked up the Tommy gun and gripped its metal barrel tightly.

I took a deep breath ready to make my run, but stopped myself at the last moment. A dim-witted thought that there might be a better way suddenly entered my head. It was risky, but one man storming a guarded ship with a Tommy gun didn't feel much better. I reached into my pocket and pulled out the lapel pin and pinned it on my overcoat collar. I stood up and took my jacket off for a moment. I lifted the Tommy gun up, slide the front handle off and dropped it in my coat pocket. I snapped the .45mm clip out and tucked it between my belt and shirt. I draped the leather strap of the gun over my shoulder and flipped the weapon around behind on my back. I stood up and put my trench coat back on concealing the gun hanging behind me. I buttoned my coat up high, straightened the rim on my hat, and started walking casually down the pier towards the boarding ramp. The two thugs at the base of the ramp saw me immediately and I saw the guns in their hands as they started running towards me. As soon as they were close enough I lifted my lapel so they could clearly see my membership pin "Strauss sent for me" I muttered calmly. They lowered their guns, nodded and motioned for me to pass by.

I headed straight for the ramp and started up towards the ship's deck. Looking back I saw the two goons retake their positions at the base of the ramp. I reached the deck, turned right and walked deliberately towards the back of the ship as if I knew just where I was going. I kept my hat down low and my overcoat buttoned up. The rain was driving hard onto the deck as two crewmen passed by me. I nodded to them and just kept walking towards the stern of the ship. I passed a large rusted out door and peered through a small porthole down into a maintenance stairway. I opened the door, stepped inside and started my way down a set of painted metal stairs.   My time in the Navy had taught me how to get around in these old tankers, and I headed straight for the engine room.

It took me about five minutes to work my way down, but I finally reached a steel door labeled Engineering. Judging by the deafening noise coming from inside, it was most likely the main engine room.   I tried at the knob, but no dice. There was an electric buzzer to the right of the door that I held down for a good ten seconds and waited. After a moment I heard hardware stirring inside the door, and suddenly the door rolled open slowly. A greasy little half balding man with sweat pouring down his face stood on the opposite side of the doorway. "Que quieres?" he questioned. I flashed my party pin to him and replied "estamos dejando poco, El capitan me pidio que ver aqui". My Spanish was a little rusty, but I hoped it would do. He turned around mumbling something to himself and headed back into the engine room.

The sound of the engines was even more deafening once I had stepped inside. The temperature was stifling… at least a hundred degrees. Sweat almost immediately started running down my head as I loosened the collar on my drenched shirt.   He led me into the core of the engine room were two weary looking men shoveled piles of coal into a boiler. "Deberia corresponder a todo vapor en unos treinta minutos." he said. I shrugged my shoulders and nodded in response, not completely understanding what he meant.

There was suddenly a loud banging noise coming from rear of the engine room. The greasy man started shouting at one of the other workers in incoherent Spanish, and the three of them staggered off down a narrow space between what appeared to be the two main engines. There was a small hatch at the end of the passage, which they passed into disappearing from my sight.

I knew I had to somehow slow them down, and quickly inventoried the grimy engine room, which was wallpapered with steam pipes and gauges. The door to the main burner was still opened, and I noticed a long crow bar hanging from one of the engines. An emergency fire hose was rolled up on the wall across from the boilers. I had to move quickly so I grabbed the crow bar and ran down the narrow passage between the engines. I slammed the hatch shut, spun the wheel, and wedged the crowbar through the handle to lock it in place. I ran back and pulled the canvas fire hose down off the wall and threw the brass end into the engine boiler. I ran back and spun the small wheel next to it, releasing high pressured water directly into the boiler. Steam gushed out of the boiler and immediately began filing the room. I bolted out of the area the same way I had entered, and closed the steel door tightly behind me. I stopped to catch my breath for a moment, and then headed back up the metal stairway, making my way topside, back onto the ship's deck. I walked outside into the driving rain, gasped a little, and took a healthy breath of the fresh ocean air.

I glanced down onto the pier, but everything was quiet with no police in sight. I lit up a cigarette and walked calmly towards the ship's mid-section. Three crew members ran by me heading in the opposite direction. I ducked behind a large shipping crate and waited in the shadows for about ten minutes. The activity on the deck started to settle down. Just then I felt the floor start to vibrate as the engines started to kick up again. A loud horn sounded above me as black smoke began pouring from the main sack positioned behind the bridge. I stepped out from the shadows and ran over to the deck railing. Several men stood on the pier at both the bow and stern preparing to cast the heavy lines off. Whatever damage I had caused hadn't lasted very long, and I needed to do something right away or I was headed for Argentina. The beaches looked nice but the politics would never agree with me.

I ripped my jacket off and swung the Tommy gun around in front of me, pulled the 30 round box magazine from under my belt and snapped it into the muzzle. I took the front handle out from my overcoat pocket, slide it onto the muzzle, and cocked back the action bolt. I ran across the deck and opened a door to the central stairway leading up to the bridge. There was nobody inside, so I slipped my shoes off and headed quietly up the stairs towards the bridge.

A large steel door with a small porthole in the upper section stood at the top of the stairway. I crouched down as I approached and peered through the glass onto the bridge. Two young sailors stood in front of a large instrument panel looking down at an array of colored lights and gauges. Off to the right was a tall slender man with greasy black hair dressed in a tattered white uniform. He was gazing out through a large set of windows that wrapped around the entire bridge. I assumed he was the ship's Captain. Standing next to him was a man I knew was Arnold Strauss. The smaller thug who had tied me up earlier was standing a few feet from the door with his back to me. I slowly turned at the door knob, and gently pushed the door open, stepping onto the bridge with my gun drawn. I let the door close on its own behind me.

The small henchman turned to see who was coming in, but it was too late for him as I slammed the wooden handle of the Tommy gun across the side of his head. It was a trick I had picked up from its previous owner. He fell hard and didn't get up.

Strauss and the Captain immediately reacted, spinning back towards me. Strauss reached his right hand inside his jacket grabbing for his gun. I quickly squeezed off a few rounds from the Tommy gun, which landed in the window to their right. He decided to withdraw his hand, as glass shattered and fell to the ground. "Hands up fellas... You don't mind if I join the party" I shouted out while pointing my gun directly at the two of them. "Now drop your guns on the ground if you don't mind, and do it slowly please." Both Strauss and the Captain slowly reached into their jackets and pulled out Luger pistols, placing them down to the ground. "Kick them over to me" I said. They did as I asked and I bent down and pocketed the guns. The two young men at the control panel stood completely motionless, looking rather nervous. I motioned to one of them "lock that door son." The young man remained still, so I tried again. "Cerrar la puerta !" He moved quickly now, bolted the door closed, and returned to the navigation panel. I turned my attention back to the Captain "English?" He looked back at me and nodded "Si." "Shut the engines down... Now!" I shouted at him.

He looked over to the two young men standing by the control panel "cerro los motores de abajo." One of the young men pulled at a lever and turned several switches off. He pushed a button and spoke into a microphone "todas las manos, las estaciones de seguridad". Within a few minutes the steady hum of engines that I had felt through the floor stopped. I shuffled the two young men away from the control panel and sat them down in a corner where I could keep an eye on them. The captain and Strauss stood stationary, shooting daggers at me with their eyes. I pulled my cigarettes out from my pocket with my free hand and slipped one out of the pack with my teeth. I pulled my lighter out and lit it up, while keeping the Tommy gun trained on Strauss. "Well folks, I think we'll all just relax for a while and wait for the police to arrive." I could tell Strauss was steaming beneath his cool exterior. Just then I heard some banging outside on the door and some muffled shouting in Spanish. I motioned for one of the young men to move, and had him stand up in front of the porthole with his hands locked behind his head.

As I turned back towards the window, I noticed the captain bent over and pulling something out of a small utility drawer. I squeezed off a quick burst, and the slugs hit him directly in his chest. He looked surprised, as a gun fell from his hand and he slumped down to the ground. I walked over and grabbed the gun from the ground "You fellas are just plain stupid! How bout you Strauss! You got any more surprises for me?" I shouted as I aimed the gun squarely at his chest. He smiled back at me "Yes Mr. Chambers. We have more surprises then you can possibly imagine. You have no idea how deep our network has seeped into your pathetic country. But very soon your pitiful government will comprehend the full force of our glorious movement." I shook my head in response "Well… it's too bad you'll never see how that works out Strauss. I can guarantee all you'll be seeing is the inside of a prison cell at San Quentin. But now that you bring it up, how about handing over those letters from the rest of your pals?" He looked back at me and laughed "I dropped those letters in the fire when we left the house tonight. Your finding them once prompted me to eliminate any evidence of our network's existence. You are free to search me if you like." Just then the sound of police sirens filled the air outside. I could hear gun fire coming from the pier. The pounding on the bridge door suddenly stopped, as footsteps retreated down the stairway.

I walked over to the bridge window and looked down onto the pier. Crew members were scattering on the deck as dozens of policeman stormed aboard the ship. The two thugs that had been guarding the boarding ramp earlier were lying bloodied and flat on their backs, no longer on guard duty. I saw Detective Bradley in a tan overcoat stepping out of a black police sedan. At least a dozen police cars with flashing lights and sirens blaring were parked on the pier. "Well, you may have destroyed the letters Strauss, but lucky for us you still have their names in that demented head of yours. I'm sure Hoover and Company will prod it out of you" I said as I started turning back around. He had his hand up in front of his face and suddenly bit down on something. I heard the sound of glass breaking inside his mouth. I flung the Tommy gun behind me, and ran towards him as he dropped to his knees. I tried to open his mouth but he had his teeth clenched tightly together. White foam began to pour out from between his teeth, and his eyes rolled back in their sockets. Within a minute he was dead. I let go of him and his lifeless body dropped to the floor. "Dam" was all I said to myself.

The pounding at the door had started again, but this time it was the good guys. I stood up and removed the lapel pin, dropping it down onto Strauss's dead body. I lifted the leather gun strap over my shoulder and placed the weapon down on the floor. I turned to the young man close to the door and motioned to him "open it".   He did as I asked and several officers rushed into the room with weapons drawn. I placed my hands over my head and stood still. One of the officers approached me while two others handcuffed the young sailors. "You Chambers?" he questioned. "Yeah" I replied calmly. "Follow me" he said as he turned and walked back off the bridge. I followed the officer out the door, down the stairway, and back out onto the main deck. The rain was still coming down heavy as he led me off the ship and down onto the pier. He guided me over to a covered loading dock where Detective Bradley stood smoking a cigarette under a small overhang. Tom motioned to the young officer "Thanks Steve, I'll take it from here." he said as the officer nodded and walked back towards the ship.

Tom turned towards me "Better give it all to me now Nick" he said. I pulled the Lugers from my pocket and handed them over to him. I took these off the captain and a man named Arnold Strauss. They're both up on that bridge, both dead. The Captain drew down on me, and Strauss chewed on a cyanide pill. Tom shot a puzzled look back at me "Cyanide?" I just shrugged my shoulders back at him. "What was their racket Nick? This doesn't seem like bootlegging to me?" he asked. "Like I said before, the ship's out of Argentina, and comes up to Providence every couple months, always making pit stops off Warwick Neck. A young lobsterman named Billing Gibson had a run in with them on more than one occasion because they were busting up his livelihood. He was the boy you pulled off the beach this past weekend. Before he died he had spoken with my missing person, who had started digging into this a few weeks ago. This outfit was dropping men at the house on Warwick Neck and running them up to Strauss's place on Blackstone Boulevard. He has a little photo processing lab up there and was manufacturing passports to help these jokers sneak into the country." Tom looked over at me again "but what's their game Nick?" he questioned. I took a cigarette out and lit it up "A fifth column for the fatherland, and Strauss was supplying the manpower and saboteurs. My client was poking around trying to find her friend Allison, and she ends up with two 9mm slugs in her head. All of these jokers are carrying 9mm Lugers. I found a stack of correspondence addressed to Strauss from addresses all over the country."

Tom pulled out a cigarette of his own and lit it "The Feds will want to get a look at those names." I shook my head and replied "No dice. Strauss destroyed everything tonight... But I did a little research on Argentina. Did you know they are one of only two countries in the Americas who haven't denounced those Nazi jokers over in Europe?" Tom shook his head as I continued. "My guess is that they've been using Argentina as a way point, and then ship their people up here as way to get sleeper agents into the states. Three of these jokers are due to sail in on October 21st, so make sure you have a welcome party waiting for them. Oh yeah, I think Allison's boss at the Journal is in with this gang, and may know the names of some of these idiots. His name is James Thompson, works in the Research Department." Tom nodded "We'll nail his ass in the morning."

Two tugs steamed by us through the channel on

their way out to guide another freighter into port. Tom looked over to me and handed me another cigarette. "I don't know Nick, it worries me. We got this crew alright, but how long have they been running this business, and how many others have already made it through the gate? I lit my cigarette and handed his lighter back over to him. "Yeah, I know what you mean" I replied. "Like an Argentine Mist we can't see, creeping its way across America and other free countries like her." I took another drag on my cigarette. The tide was coming in now and the rain was starting to subside a little. "These Nazi jokers are trying to muscle in on Uncle Sam, but sooner or later they're going to have to crawl out from whatever rock they've been hiding under, and when they do they won't know what hit them."

Tom blew some smoke out from his mouth "I hope your right Nick... I sure hope your right." he replied. "So that raps it up for you. Your client and the missing person killed by this mob for meddling in their operation?" I stared out at the ocean for a moment. "This crew killed my client alright, but they didn't kill Allison. Half a dozen stab wounds to the gut? That's just too personal, and these clowns were total business." Tom shook his head a little "Then what about the Baxter Girl?" he asked. I looked back at him "I've got one more stop to make tonight and I should have that answer for you." He shook his head and took a long slow drag on his cigarette "Ok Nick, I'll give you a little rope tonight, but find that last piece of the puzzle. Just make dam sure you're down at the station first thing in the morning to fill out a complete report." He flicked his cigarette into the water, turned his back to me and began walking back out towards his car. Just then I remembered my gas situation and spun back towards him "Hey, how about a lift?" He opened the door to his car and looked over the roof back at me "Sure, where to?" I threw my butt down on the pavement and replied "Federal Hill".

19: Back to the Hill

Ten minutes later Tom was dropping me off on Atwells Avenue. I stepped out of the car and he leaned over the seat towards the open door "Do I even want to ask what you're doing here? "See you first thing on the morning Tom" I replied as I closed the door behind me and started walking up Federal Hill while he drove off. I came to the two story tenement house at 119 Atwells Ave, and headed up the driveway. Corrao had given me twenty-four hours and I was returning a day late, which was never a good thing with these mob guys.

As I approached the back yard, the same two Italian men I saw two nights earlier were still posted next to the garage smoking cigarettes. They dropped their buts when then saw me walk up, quickly drew their guns and ran towards me. I held my hands up "I need to see your boss." One of the men shoved me face first up against the house and began searching me, while the second man ran up the back stairway. The first man finished searching me and turned me around. He held the gun to my chest while we waited for the second man to come back down with an answer. Two minutes passed and we finally heard footsteps coming back down the stairs. The other man came out and pointed his revolver up the stairway "Andiamo!" he said. I walked in front of him and started up the back stairway. When we reached the second floor I opened the door to the kitchen and began heading through it. He gave me a little nudge in my ribs with his revolver, and I kept moving straight through into the living room. On the opposite wall there was an open door that led out to a small porch, which looked down onto Atwells Avenue. He shoved my shoulder in that direction and I walked outside onto the second story porch.

Corrao was seated at a small wooden fold-up table drinking a glass of red wine and smoking a Cuban cigar. A half empty gallon of wine sat on the table along with one unused wine glass. He looked over at me "Bounasera... Well you got a set of balls if nothing else Chambers. I'll give you that. Sit down, qualche vino." I did as he said and sat down next to him at the table. He took another sip from his glass and looked down at the passing traffic. A few horns sounded below, while the wind blew a light mist from the rain up onto the porch.   He turned his attention back towards me "When did I tell you to get back to me Chambers? Maybe it's my memory failing, but I don't think it was tonight. I try to be a gentleman and give you some time to do your job, but what do I hear from you yesterday? Niente! That ain't right Chambers." He paused for a moment and then continued on "Imagine my surprise when I get call from a friend down at the station saying they found Allison's body in some scummy alleyway with half a dozen knife wounds in her stomach. Che Diavolo!" His voice began to escalate in volume as he stood up from the chair. "I'll tell you what I was thinking. I was thinking where's the shamus? Why hasn't he called to check in? Maybe I should just send a few of the boys out to pump some lead in his chest! That's what I was thinking Chambers" I took my hat off and pulled at my right ear lobe before responding "I've got some answers now… I didn't have them until tonight, and I didn't want to come to you with half a story." Corrao sat down slowly, opened the gallon of wine, poured a glass and handed it over to me.

"Say whatever it is you came here to say Chambers, and you had better hope I like your story. Cause whoever did that to Allison is going to get pay back from me a hundred times over.   If you ain't got, well let's just satisfactory answers for me now, then I think we'll just take some of that payback out on you. So start chatting." He lifted a .45 automatic from his lap for me to see and placed it on the table with his hand over it.

I nodded, picked up the glass of wine, wet my palette, and started in with my story. "Charlotte was killed by a mob working out of the East Side. Only this wasn't your ordinary run of the mill crew. Their racket was smuggling foreign agents into America on a ship named the Argentine Mist. She's down in the Port of Providence right now being searched by the police. Their Captain is lying dead up on the bridge because I shot him. The ship was dropping this gang of socialist monkeys off at a house on Warwick Neck, and printing off passports and other necessary papers over at a place on the East Side. Then they would send them off on their merry way to start a fifth column for Uncle Adolph, while wreaking havoc on Uncle Sam." Corrao shrugged his shoulders and shot me a look of disbelief "What are you trying to say Chambers? It was a bunch of Nazi's who killed Allison?" he started laughing "Chambers, when I said you had balls, I didn't know the half of it."

He rubbed his eyes a little, and I kept talking "You told me Allison was doing some research on fish migration out on Narragansett Bay, so I decided to look into that. Three weeks ago she was doing some research down at Oakland Beach and interviewed a young lobsterman named Billy Gibson. He told Allison he was having problems with a large freighter that was pulling out from the channel near Warwick Neck and dredging up his lobster pots. It was the same freighter that the police are rummaging through down at the Shipyard right now. Allison decided to do some investigating on the kid's behalf and had a tiff with the Ship's Captain a couple of weeks ago. Well, this mob didn't like the attention she was giving them, so they grabbed her about a week ago and stashed her up on the East Side. The kid ended washing up on the beach Saturday morning. On Thursday night

Allison escaped and made her way to a friend's house. The friend said she left on Friday, and hasn't seen her since."

It looked like I was starting to get Corrao's attention "Where did she go on Friday?" he asked. "Her friend said she was headed to my office, but she never showed" I replied. He took out his lighter and relit his half smoked Cuban. "Is that all of it?" he questioned in an unsatisfied tone. I looked back over at him "No, the friend said one of your people was picking her up and taking her to my office." He stood up immediately "Who was it?" I shook my head "She wasn't sure, just said Allison had called here to ask for your help, and someone who worked for you was coming to pick her up." He sat back down and thought for a moment "It doesn't make sense Chambers. I never got any call from Allison? If one of my men is behind what happened to Allison, he won't be breathing for much longer. We'll find out who it was and take care of things our own way." He pulled a second cigar out of his pocket and handed it to me. I took out a match and lit it.

I waited a minute or so before speaking again "How close were you to Charlotte? I know you said you dated for a while, but how serious did it get?" He shrugged his shoulders a little "We dated for maybe a year or so, but it was never exclusive." I puffed on the smooth Cuban "She was digging up information in the same sandboxes I was playing in. Chances are she caught the attention of that mob, so they decided put two 9mm slugs in her head, and dump her body behind that warehouse down by the shipyard. Did she know Allison?" He looked up at me before responding "Si, magari. I'm sure they bumped into each other down at the club." "How did it end with you two?" I asked. "If I remember right, the dame was a little put off at first. You know how it is, but she got over it in time. I started seeing Allison and she moved on. Why all the personal questions Chambers?" he asked with a sense of frustration.

"You hired Charlotte to find Allison..." I paused for a moment. "Well maybe she did. Allison's friend Liz said whoever she spoke with worked for you and was on their way to pick her up. Charlotte worked for you. It's true, maybe dancing down in a club, but Allison knew she worked for you and that may have been good enough for her. Let's say Allison couldn't reach you at your apartment, so she calls the club looking for you. Charlotte picks up the telephone, and let's Allison know she'll be right over to pick her up. She already has an appointment with me, so she tells Allison I can probably help and that she should go with her to meet with me at my office. She may have even said you were meeting us there...

The problem is that five o'clock rolls around and

only Charlotte shows up at my place, and she's still playing your act out for me. Why? She was late getting there, she was shaken, and she looked as though she had been out in the rain for some time. She told me she walked three blocks in the rain, when most of the city had already cleared out. Why would she want to do that? Coincidently, Allison was found about three blocks from my office." I looked over at Corrao. The gears in his head were turning now. He had an empty stare and his face showed no emotion whatsoever. I decided to keep talking "Do you have a kitchen down at your club?" He nodded. "Well, let's have someone check to see if a ten inch ivory handle carving knife is missing?" Corrao looked up at the goon still standing guard in the doorway "controllo su di esso!" he said as he motioned to the man with his cigar.

The man walked off and soon I heard the sound of heavy footsteps heading down the back stairs. I kept going "Some women hold grudges, just can't seem to let things go. Charlotte may have had a beef with Allison for causing your breakup. She probably thought the two of you wouldn't last, but maybe when she saw it was heating up over the past few months she knew she had to do something. That phone call from Allison may have been her opportunity. She knew Allison was already in some kind of trouble, maybe the kind that could get her killed. She knew you were worried enough to hire me to try and find her, and maybe you were already expecting the worse. She must have been pretty disappointed when she heard Allison's voice over that phone. Let's just say she picks up Allison, takes her downtown, but not to my office. She takes her three blocks back into a dingy alleyway and points over to old stairwell she claims is my basement office. Allison steps to the top, and Charlotte thrusts the blade into her kidney. She falls forward, cracks her head up against the brick wall, landing face up at the base of the stairwell. But Charlotte wants to be sure she never gets up. She walks down the stairway and sticks her six more times in the gut until she's sure. Then maybe she decides to walk back several blocks to my office to clear her head, or maybe it's just to let the rain wash the blood off her jacket... Who really knows with these cold blooded types?" Corrao cut me off at that point "Basta! I get the picture Chambers." Just then the tall man emerged back out onto the deck. He nodded his head "Yeah boss, Cook says we've been missing one of the good carving knives for the past few days. He thinks one of the staff might have stolen it."

Corrao put his cigar down into the ashtray, and poured himself a little more homemade wine. "Well, it looks like I can thank those Argentine assholes for offing that crazy broad. She would have gotten a lot worse if I had found her first." He picked the .45 up off the table and pointed it at me for a few seconds before lowering it back down onto his lap. "Our man down at the station said you kept me out of it. That bought you some chips with me. How you gonna leave it with them?" I stood up, turned to lean over the porch rail, and looked down at the street below "Oh... pretty much the same story I guess, except I'm thinking Charlotte was just a friend of Allison's." He drank a little more wine "Well, then I guess I'm Ok with letting you walk outta here tonight. Not much you coulda done to save Allison. Sounds like she was dead before you even took the job to find her... Even so, not so bad work on your part Chambers. A little slow, but you got there eventually! If you weren't a stinking Irishman, I'd offer you a job." I laughed a little "That's ok. I've gotten pretty comfortable being in the poorhouse. I'm not really sure if my system could adjust to a different lifestyle at my age.

He reached into his jacket pocket, pulled out five one hundred dollar bills and tossed them on the table. "Maybe you try it for a little while" he suggested. I looked down at the cash on the table "Thanks anyway, but I've already been well paid for this job. Like I said, I wouldn't even know what to do with it." He nodded his head and I started to walk out off the porch, but decided to turn around at the last moment. "I would like to ask one favor?" He looked up at me and replied "Go ahead... ask away." I leaned up against the door jamb for a moment. "I was wondering if you might still have some influence with Vincent Palaeno?" I asked. He lit his cigar again "Forse… why?" I pulled at my right ear a little "Well, we banged heads a bit on this case. Let's just say I don't want to walk out for the paper one morning and have my head bashed in with a baseball bat." He laughed a little and let the cigar smoke drifted up casually out from his mouth "I'll talk with him." "Thanks!" I replied as I shook his hand and walked off the porch.

20: Lobster Traps

I slept late on Tuesday morning. My eyes opened up around 9:00am as I pushed up my bedroom window and took a look outside. It was a beautiful autumn day. The sky was clear and the sun was completely in charge now. I got up, took a shower, and called a cab to take me back to my car at the Ship Yard. I brought along some gasoline to put in the tank and then headed right down to the station to give my statement to Tom and the Captain. I gave them pretty much the same story I had given Corrao the night before with a few minor adjustments. The police wouldn't mind either way because it all added up nicely from their perspective. Everything fit into a nice neat box, which is the way they usually liked things. The Captain had a press conference scheduled right after our meeting, where he credited the Providence Police Department for exposing a major espionage ring operating in Rhode Island. My name wasn't mentioned, but that's how things usually went in my line of work. As I was strolling out of the building, I noticed two officers and a federal agent walking James Thompson into the station in handcuffs. That was good news. Maybe they could squeeze a few names out of him before he got the chair for treason.

I stopped at the newsstand and picked up the morning paper. I hesitantly asked the kid for a pack of Lucky Strike "Yes sir, just got some in today" he replied. "One pack mister?" I smiled back at him "Make it three please." He handed them over to me and I happily paid him adding a nice tip for his trouble.

I made a quick stop by the Journal to break the news to Elizabeth Brennan. It didn't go well. After that I jumped into my car and headed south for Oakland Beach. Twenty minutes later I was pulling up to the pier at Brush Neck Cove. I parked my car and walked up onto the dock, making my way down towards the Misty Blue. The water seemed much calmer today, and its color was a clear ocean blue. A light ripple could be seen on the water's surface, as a gentle breeze pushed itself over the dock. Dozens of Seagulls flew overhead squawking at me, while I let the fresh ocean air fill my polluted lungs.

I approached the Gibson boat "Ahoy, anyone aboard?" One of the cabin doors opened, and the old man stuck his head out from inside "Hello friend, please step aboard" he replied. I did as he said and jumped onto the boat. "Just made a pot of coffee, can I interest you young man?" he asked. "Sure thing" I replied as I sat down on the side of the boat. A minute later he emerged with two cups of black coffee with no sugar or cream. I took one of the cups from him "Thanks! How are you doing Mr. Gibson?" He took a seat in the Captain's chair, looked back at me and smiled "Within tolerance Mr. Chambers… within tolerance. I'm still breathing in this fresh sea air, so I can't complain that much. How about yourself? Did you ever find what you where after?" I looked up at him "Yes… we sure did, and I can tell you they won't be bothering anyone anymore." He turned back at me and smiled again "Well, that's some good news. I thank you for that young man." I pulled out a cigarette and lit one up "There is something important I need to let you know. That mob out on the tanker wasn't your ordinary crew, and they weren't just dredging up lobster pots. They had bigger plans, including sabotage and undermining Uncle Sam. If Billy hadn't stirred things up with those boys, a lot of innocent people would have been hurt. I'm not sure if that helps, but I just thought you should know."

He turned back towards the control panel and looked out over the bow. "Actually, that does help. Thanks again Nick. Now how about casting off that bow line for me, and let me show you how we catch lobster." He turned the key on the ignition. Two puffs of smoke lifted out of the water as the boat's twin engines turned over. I cast off the bow line and walked back to the stern. I held the boat in place until the old man gave me the signal and then jumped aboard, releasing the line from the dock cleat. He gunned the engine and we motored off out onto the Bay.

Argentine Mist

By Christopher Dacey

 Visit us on FaceBook under *Argentine Mist*

Contact Author at chrisdacey@yahoo.com

Front Cover Photo : Aruba Coastline – C. Dacey

Inside Cover Photo, Rhode Island Coastline – G. Scagliarini

CPSIA information can be obtained at www.ICGtesting.com
Printed in the USA

242366LV00001B/21/P